The Last Cowboy

by

Jan Herrman

TELEMACHUS PRESS

Cover designed by Telemachus Press, LLC

Cover art:
Copyright © iStock-471966603_Neutronman
Copyright © iStock-1145983808_subinpumsom

Maps:
Copyright © iStock-1125032402_ZU_09
Copyright © iStock-871166960_bgblue
Copyright © ShutterStock 98504378_Nicku

Publishing Services by Telemachus Press, LLC
7652 Sawmill Road
Suite 304
Dublin, Ohio 43016
http://www.telemachuspress.com

ISBN 978-1-951744-85-4 (eBook)
ISBN 978-1-951744-86-1 (paperback)

Library of Congress Control Number: 2021922149

Version 2021.12.31

Dedication

For my wife Marta, prettiest cowgirl in the West

Acknowledgments

I want to thank the folks at Telemachus for the extraordinary amount of time and invaluable guidance they provided, especially Steve Himes and Karen Lieberman. Their patience with an anxious author was greatly appreciated. And I would be extraordinarily remiss if I did not also thank my volunteer editors Rebecca Bloom, Rick Hudson, Marty and Alice Bauman, as well as a very special one, Marta Herrman.

To Jane and Ira,

I hope you enjoy!

Table of Contents

Maps

Texas

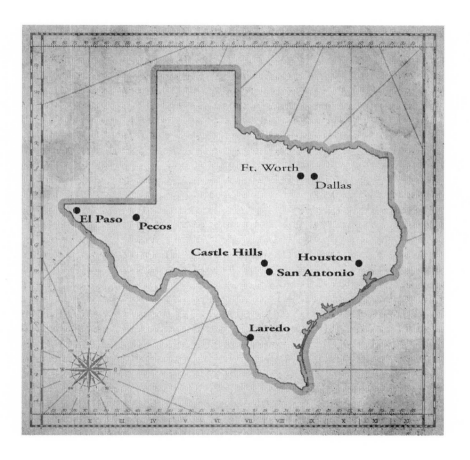

Morocco

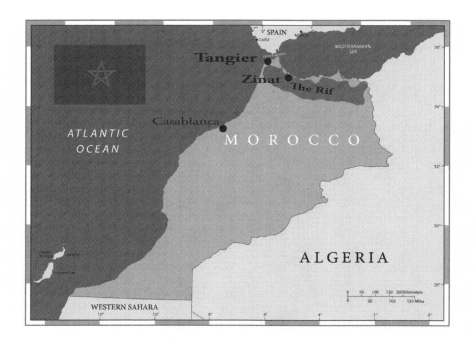

San Francisco

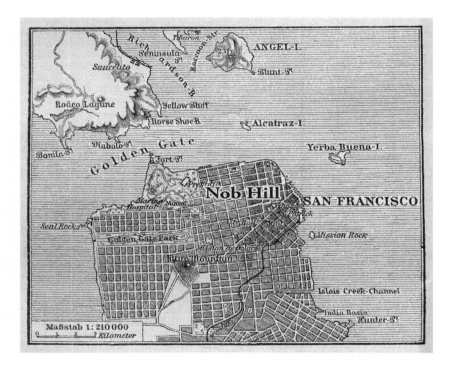

Prologue

I've done a lot of things in my life that I'm not right proud of. But I sure am proud of reading my first long book. It's called *Lord Jim*. Like him, I stand short of six feet. In fact, I am a hair or two shorter than five foot eight. And this is my first piece of writing. So, I keep my Webster's as close as I used to keep my Colt. I surely don't want to shame myself with poor spelling.

Beth had me read *Walden; Or, A Life in the Woods* a month before. It was a short book. That's why I count *Lord Jim* as my first long one. I am not like Mr. Thoreau. I never wanted to hide myself away anywhere. I never found the calm he did in solitude. And I did not have a mother to wash my clothes. Once I got the hang of acquiring things, I did not want to give them up. I guess I don't measure up to his standards.

Beth told me to begin this expository with something I know about. She told me that was me. Like I said, I'm not proud of all what I done. I don't always credit myself as someone worthy of a story. But I do admit that I led what them newspaper boys call a colorful life. If I took a guess, I'd say I painted that empty canvas with more colors than Joseph had in his coat. It's just that not all of it is good.

The Last Cowboy

Chapter 1:
Nob Hill, San Francisco. November 4, 1893

(Nineteen Years Earlier or Thereabouts. The Past)

Charlie Sets Me Straight

When I was 16, I ran with a border gang in West Texas, near El Paso. It was 1873. I was sowing my wild oats. I wanted adventure. The folks I rode with weren't such bad fellas. They never killed nobody, at least most of them didn't, except Mr. Clement. He could be a hard man, yes he could. But I never personally saw him shoot anyone. We were what you might call equal opportunity thieves. Sometimes, we'd ride across the shallows of the Rio Grande into Mexico and rustle us up some cattle to sell once back on the American side. Other times we did our rustling on the Texas side and sell them longhorns to Mexicans. I admit, it got a-might confusing, trying to keep track of who to steal from and who to sell to. It also got a-might dangerous being shot at from both sides of the border. No matter the source of our ill-gotten gains, we would always celebrate a safe return with whatever alcoholic beverage we had on hand.

Our camp had two old shacks, a solitary windmill and a corral for our straggily mounts. Looking back, it was a hard-scrabble life. I didn't know no better. I was shot at more times than I could count. I was lucky, I guess, that I never was hit. Come to think of it, I been a lucky fella most all my life.

It was the Ake brothers that taught me to shoot. They was with us for a short while, until they moved on to make a real name for themselves. I hear tell they killed a lot of folks and came to a bad end. But for some reason they took a liking to me and took me under their wing. Whenever I had the chance, I pretended to be a real gunslinger just like them, practicing my fast draw. I sure used up a lot of bullets shooting cans off the fence posts around the corral. The other members of our gang never took too kindly to the racket I made with all that gun play and what they saw as a waste of good slugs. I must have amused them enough with all my playacting to tolerate the noise. I came to be a passable shot.

Jeff Ake, himself, led me out of a life of crime. He had been a lawman once, going back and forth across that border which separated the legal from the illegal. His word, though, still held some weight in the lawman community. He took me into El Paso one day and introduced me to the local Wells Fargo agent. It turns out he was a-looking for a man to ride shotgun for the run out to Pecos. Neither of us said that I never did nothing like that before. Jeff vouched for me, and there I was sitting in that top seat the next day, shotgun in hand.

It was a long run, leaving at seven sharp every third Tuesday morning. Take us seven days, it would, to reach Pecos and seven back. Other stages would take passengers and cargo on from there to other parts of Texas and beyond.

Old Charlie Breen was the driver. He was twice my age and looked near four times it. His beard had gone grey, and I swear he must have been missing half his teeth. He sure liked his whiskey, but never drank at work. Never. It was a strict rule for him. He lived by the rules and taught me to do the same. He taught me more than that. He showed me how to carry myself in public, how to make sure I always looked presentable. (I had forgotten how to behave in what I now come to think of as my outlaw days.)

In fact, I remember the very first time we met outside the Wells Fargo Office. It was like yesterday. His first words to me were, "You smell like wild, boy. Where you been liv'n? Among a pack of horses? Gone to horse, have you?"

"Listen mister, I'm not a boy. I got a name, too. And it's not boy. I'm Hank, Hank Miller." Never mind I barely had a whisker or two on my face.

Charlie chose to overlook that fact and not pursue the boy angle. "Well Mister Hank Miller, I'm not going to sit atop that stage until you get yourself a bath and a clean set of clothes. I strongly advise you burn them ones you got on."

"I ain't got no money."

"Any money."

"That's what I said. I ain't got no money."

"I'll loan it to you. It's worth the investment."

I did what he said. It was the first, but not the last time.

He and I became close friends after that. Charlie had never married. He did carry a locket in his vest pocket. Old Charlie had a sweetheart who died of the smallpox. He would cry over sweet Sue after downing not a few number of swigs. I always felt a little embarrassed at those times and a lot sad. He was a good man and deserved better. But I learned early in life that folks don't always get what they deserve. We would never speak about it the next day.

Well, it was two-and-a-half days out when it happened. I'll always remember that day until I die, the third of May it was, in the year 1878. We were rounding a bend we had passed dozens of times. Them bushwhackers came out of nowhere, shooting and a-hollering loud enough you'd think it was midnight in a Dodge City saloon. There were four of them. Charlie reined in the horses, since two of those no accounts were blocking the road. The other two rode alongside. He nudged me to set down the scatter gun, knowing there was nothing I could do to fight off all four. That was the last thing I remembered. When I awoke I was lying in the dirt. My head hurt, and I couldn't see straight. I sat up and saw a pool of blood on the ground about where my head had been. I touched the left side of my skull and found the crease. I was lucky, I guess. I tried to get up but fell right back down, dizzy as a fox-chased chicken. Well, I finally got myself up and found them. All three of the passengers lie dead in the dusty ground, each full of bullet holes. I found Charlie on the other side of the carriage, just as dead as the others. The empty strong box with the lock shot off was next to him. I am not ashamed to say that I shed lonely tears. I had no tools to bury them; so I said a prayer to have the Lord take their souls.

I was mad, madder than I had ever been in my entire life. It was the anger that got me focused. I set aside the pain that felt like it would split my head in two and got myself moving. By the look of the sun it was near noon. I knew what I was going to do. I unhitched the horses and sent two of them on their way. They would most likely wander back to the nearest station house. I kept two for myself. I gathered up our canteens and put two of them crosswise on my chest. I picked up the scatter gun, stuck Charlie's six shooter into my gun belt, and mounted one of the horses. I took that locket out of his vest and put it in my pocket. Those vultures picked their victims clean before they left, but somehow missed the locket. Too small, I guess. I've kept it ever since. I was going to find them killers and give them the buckshot they deserved.

Setting off bareback with another horse in tow was no easy thing. But I managed. Their trail was easy to follow. They must have figured that no one was going to come a-looking for them. They was wrong.

By nightfall I saw a campfire I reckon was about ten miles east of the ambush. I dismounted, left the horses tied to a bush and slowly approached. Well, I found them. They was passing around a jug of whiskey, whooping, and staring into that fire. It made 'em night blind that fire did. They wasn't just killers. They was stupid, lazy killers.

I crept up on them. And suddenly they all came into a strangely clear focus. I saw nothing but them. All else was blotted out. They became targets, that's all they were. I came a-running out of the brush like the avenging madman I was.

I paid no heed to danger, not because I was courageous, but because I was angry. Angry enough to kill.

I pulled both triggers on that shotgun and watched as the two sitting on the other side of the campfire were blown backwards. I took out both of my guns and kept firing until they were empty. It seemed that neither of the other two even moved. I don't know how many bullet holes I found in the man lying dead in front of me.

The fourth had run off. I saw a trail of blood in the dim light of the fire, reloaded and went off after him. Thinking back, this was not a right smart thing to do in the dark. He could be out there ready to ambush me, bushwhacker that he was. I should have waited until sunrise. But my blood was up, and I was too young to know better. And I was lucky. I was always lucky.

I found him, dead, not two hundred yards from the campsite. I spit on his body and turned back. I said earlier that folks don't always get what they deserve, leastways in this life. It was true of Charlie and those poor passengers. But I was wrong about them four murderers. They got just what they deserved.

When I returned to their camp it was nearly dawn. I saw the men and the blood, and I was sick. I never killed no one before. I ain't ashamed to say I vomited, until my belly spasmed with pain. Then, I fell to the ground so tired that I fell asleep right there.

By time I woke it was late in the day. I saddled all four of their horses and slung each dead man over them. I don't know where I got the strength from. Then I put the saddle-bags containing the stolen cash up there with them. I knew I had to return that money. It wasn't mine to keep. I could not tolerate stealing any of it, not one dollar. No sir. That would put me in the company of the same criminals who had killed my friend Charlie. I do recall eating hardtack and jerky before setting back out for El Paso. What made me bring them killers in I don't rightly know. Some instinct, I guess. It was a day-and-a-half before I reached town with only dead men as company. A crowd gathered as I rode in. Even in that wild border town, a man leading five horses with bodies lying atop four of them was not a common sight.

The sheriff was calmly sitting in a chair outside his office, seemingly unperturbed by the ruckus. Thank the Lord he recognized me right off. As he got up all he said was, "Looks like you ran into a pack of trouble Hank. I guess you took care of it. Where's Charlie and the stage." I told him.

Old Bill Coke went inside and came back out with a stack of wanted posters in his hands. He lifted the head of each robber by the hair and compared them to the drawings. I remember to this day his exact words, "Looks like you got yourself a reward coming. That one there calls himself Cole the Younger Younger, seeing as how he is, er, was the younger brother of Cole. He had a thousand dollars on his head." Sheriff Coke sure liked to start off anything he said with, "Looks like."

"That one there is Joe Bass, younger brother of Sam. He'll come after you for sure. Looks like you bought yourself a real passel of trouble, along with all that reward money, Hank." He was right. But I was always lucky.

Chapter 2:
Nob Hill, San Francisco. May 7, 1912

(Nineteen Years Later or Thereabouts. The Present)

The Letter

T he letter arrived at eight in the morning. It arrived by bicycle messenger. A rail strike had temporarily halted mail delivery in San Francisco. Its contents would alter the course of a nation.

Hank Miller answered the door, took the envelope, and tipped the rider ten cents. It was a battered piece of work, that envelope, torn in spots and post mark unreadable. There was no return address. Nevertheless, he immediately knew who the sender was. Hank stood in his elaborate foyer, filled with fine mahogany furniture, topped in places by Victorian lamps. There was an ancient vase with oriental decoration in one corner, standing tall, a miniature sentry to guard the household. All those who entered would need to pass that centuries old watchman. Sunlight filtered in through the stained glass of the front door, casting a multicolored array on the pink marble floor.

Hank called out to Beth, "Honey, it's a letter from Ali." Elizabeth failed to immediately reply, occupied as she was, reading *Moby Dick* for the third time.

"Open it Hank. What does he have to say?"

He brought it to the parlor where Beth sat in her most comfortable burgundy colored velvet-covered chair. Hank marveled at his good fortune at marrying this woman. He had often asked himself why she had chosen him. Yes, she was beautiful. She was also educated and refined and smart. She was the one who saw to his education. He might never have been a ruffian, but he was certainly rough behind the edges before she had taken a gentle file to those bristly parts. Some stubble remained, though, waiting for an untamed moment to grow back. Maybe that was a good thing for what lay ahead. Hank broke his reverie to read aloud.

January 12, 1912
Zinat, Morocco

Dear Hank,

It has been too long since we have traded letters. The fault is not mine. Hasan Al-Aziz, may he dwell in heaven, died almost 2 years ago. His oldest son, Ahmed, took control of tribal leadership. Many persons risked their lives to send this letter to you. I am no longer general. Ahmed has banished me from his army. I live with my daughter Amina in a tent outside the palace. My Layla is dead from the consumption.

I am watched all the time. There is nowhere to go. Ahmed was always jealous of his father's affection toward me. He has made me nothing. He lets me live a life of poverty and shame as a warning to all those who would oppose him. I was loyal to his family. I was and still am. I owe his revered father everything. If I were not so desperate, I would never have sent this letter to you. I must protect Amina. I fear for her life. She must not grow up this way. Please come.

Your friend for all time. With great respect,
Ali

They were both stunned. Beth tensed, fearing her husband's reaction. She was tough, really tough, as events had clearly shown. But she knew her husband all too well and feared losing him.

It came as no surprise to either of them when he began, "Beth, I owe him. You know that. Without Ali there would be no us, no David or Ben or Rachael, no nothing. I'd be lying in an unmarked grave six thousand miles away."

"I know, Hank."

There was no point in arguing. She knew he would go. The problem was developing a viable rescue plan. That letter was almost five months old. Ali and his daughter could be dead by now for all they knew. Neither of them would go to the office that morning.

They sat down for a breakfast of porridge, sweetened with honey and sprinkled with strawberries. Stress never seemed to dim his appetite. Leaving his family for a far-off land and the perils it held would be a painful choice. Hank had vowed to never do so. His sole aim had been to be a devoted husband and father. But he was drawn to duty as much as any soldier. Hank had lived a wild, nomadic life and wanted no more than the contentment he had found with Beth and the children.

Beth for her part hardly touched her food. She feared for their future. Their present had become reliably comfortable. She did not want that comfort disturbed. The prospect of losing Hank was unbearable. She had seen the very real dangers the world held: the evil people kept stored in their hearts and the fury the earth kept buried deep within.

***

San Francisco had recently recovered from an enormous earthquake and the devastating fire that followed. It occurred six years ago. Hank and Elizabeth had contributed to that recovery with their time and money. Despite their efforts and those of many others, an undercurrent of uncertainty remained. The memory of so many lives lost or disrupted lurked beneath the consciousness of the city. It affected them, too, a reminder that fate was often unkind, even to the righteous. Their family had been lucky. Their home had been untouched, and their business was thriving.

They had come to San Francisco in 1893. The twins, David Solomon and Benjamin William, followed less than a year later. David was named for no one in particular. Hank said it sounded like a strong name for a strong boy. And the addition of Solomon would bestow wisdom. First to be born, he would represent a fresh start for all of them without any link to the shackles of Hank's past, at least as far as his name was concerned. But as they both knew, in reality, you could not escape your past. It was with you always, for good or evil. His junior twin, Ben, joined the world eighteen minutes after his older brother. He was named for his maternal grandfather Benjamin Joseph Franklin. Rachael Anne was born in 1895, honoring both Elizabeth's grandmother, Rachael Agnes Astor and Hank's mother.

Shortly after their arrival in the city, they opened *The American West Tour Company* in an office at Main and Broad. It was an immediate success, attracting the well-healed, first from California and later from the rest of the world. Hank had started the business from an office in San Antonio, almost six years before settling in San Francisco. He had begun by arranging tours of the "Olde Wild West," advertising in newspapers across the country and beyond. He had his routes well planned to take clients on three and four-day excursions into the picturesque Hill Country outside of town.

Hank always began at the Alamo with a scripted narrative. He continued on through a rapidly changing landscape of desert, green valleys, hills, forests and streams. It was populated by wild animals that folks from the cities of the East had seen only in photos or drawings. And the land was decorated by a surprising array of plant life, which seemed to bloom exclusively for his guests. Hank told stories of the old West, regaling the tourists with desperados and the lawmen who chased them down. He even had locals play the role of bad guys he would scare away from camp.

After the headquarters moved to San Francisco, the little tour company grew into a worldwide phenomenon, ultimately offering excursions for Americans to the cities and towns of Europe and Europeans to America. They established offices in New York, Chicago, and London. They even acquired their own passenger ships to ferry customers back and forth across the Atlantic. A rival company called the *International Express Tours* had proposed a merger to create the largest travel business in the world. It would surpass even *Thomas Cook* of England. The new entity would take part of its name, *American*, from Hank and Elizabeth's enterprise, and *Express* from theirs.

Although it might have been built with the silver of nearby mines, San Francisco now attracted business of all types. Wells Fargo established its headquarters there. Bank of America would follow a decade later. Levi Strauss had long ago opened his dry goods store. Cable cars had been in operation for two decades. The area known as the Barbary Coast had been cleared of criminals. Well, mostly so. At least it was uncommon now to be robbed, murdered or shanghaied if you ventured into the area. Wealthy residents of the cities, including San Francisco itself, wanted to experience what they read had been an exciting era of the American frontier. The authors of the dime store novel had done the work of advertising for Hank. If his clients had known what really had taken place, they might not have gone on those tours in the first place. Hank and Beth knew. They had lived it. But in its earliest stages the business, before it expanded, depended on selling a legend, and that they did well.

For Hank and Beth, their *Wild West Tour* remained the most popular. Aspiring cowboys from around the globe lined up in droves to be able to set out on the trails of the frontier. They did their best to simulate an authentic experience. There were times he missed the dusty prairies and green hills and rivers and brilliant night sky of his native state. Those times were fleeting. His family and his adopted city always drew him home.

***

"I never thought to return, not in my wildest dreams. We have a lot to discuss."

"Well, Hank, I know what you want to do, I guess what you must do. I know better than to argue with you. Let's get the children together and decide. Call the office and tell them we won't be in today." Her husband was a man of honor. He would keep his word, even if it meant he died trying. That thought lanced through her chest as if she had been truly stabbed.

The dueling commitments tore at him. He valued family above all else, but he owed his life to a man who lived thousands of miles away. In point of fact Ali might not still be living at all.

David and Ben came back from the downtown office. They were home for the summer from their third year at Harvard. Both were history majors and thought they were headed to law school. Fate had something else in store for them. They were tall, six feet each, and dwarfed their father. The boys were handsome fellas and a little too aware of it, if truth be told. They had the broad shoulders of the athletes they were. The young ladies of Radcliffe had taken notice.

Rachael was sitting at the dining room table when they came in through the front door. She was bound for Swarthmore in the fall. It had been founded as a Quaker college, now nonsectarian and coeducational and, most importantly, her mother's alma mater. She would live with her grandparents in Philadelphia. At seventeen, she had the rich black hair of her mother and the emerald green eyes of her father. She was a stunning beauty, something Hank gave his wife all the credit for.

The brothers spoke at the same time, as they often did, "Where's mom and pops?"

"Here in a minute."

They took seats across from one another. They had learned it was best to separate themselves a bit. Otherwise, people, including their parents, could not always tell who was doing the talking. Their voices were so similar that without looking directly at one or the other, you couldn't always tell who said what. However, since they often said the same thing, it didn't always seem to matter. Elizabeth and Hank had long ago given up trying to tell them apart. The running joke, which had lost steam over the years because they had used it so often, was to address either or both of them as BenDavid.

As they entered the room Hank could not resist, "Howdy there boys, BenDavid." Rachael moaned at the worn dad joke even though it equally belonged to her mother.

"Pops, what's this all about?" one of the two twins asked. It had come from Ben, the junior partner of the duo.

The three siblings sat silently after Hank explained the situation, not sure how to react. Rachael was the first to stake her claim, "Whatever we work out, I'm going."

In unison, the other four reflexively replied, "Oh no you're not."

"I can shoot daddy's old Henry with the best of you. In fact, I've beaten you all at target practice so many times I can't count. You go ahead and deny it. You know it's true. Like Daddy used to say, I 'can shoot the eye out of a racoon at two hundred paces'."

"Honey, it's too dangerous," Hank knew he was entering dangerous territory.

"You mean too dangerous for a girl, right? You both always told me to be whatever I want to be. Well, I want to *be* wherever you are going."

That stumped them for a minute, until Beth spoke up. "Rachael, the only place you are going is Philadelphia. There is no further discussion on this point. However, you will take part in the planning of the operation. We need your insight."

Everyone assembled at the table knew that tone. Their mother rarely used it. They knew that the decision was final. It was not to be questioned. And they were mightily relieved.

Rachael, not quite ready to surrender, decided on a different tack, knowing this last gasp was almost certainly futile. "How could I possibly study, knowing the three of you were in so much danger?" She conveniently ignored the fact that, if all went well, the three men would be home for the start of the fall semester.

"What do you mean three of you? There's four of us," immediately came from Elizabeth. "You need me to watch your back," she said, directing her gaze at her husband. "I saved you once. I might need to do it again." That had always been a matter of marital debate.

Now it was Hank's turn. "Now hold on, all of you. We first have to decide if *I* am going anywhere. Then we can figure out who goes where." He was holding onto Charlie's locket in his pants pocket with his left hand. He already knew he had to go. The question was whether one or both of the boys would go with him. He would hang onto the rest of his ammunition to be discussed later in private with Beth. He would keep his powder dry, so to speak, until then. They had already passed the look between them. This argument would not be held in front of their children. He already knew what he would have to say, and she knew it too. It would have to be said aloud, but when they were alone and could hold each other. Beth would stay behind in case things didn't turn out well. Someone had to be there for Rachael.

"Hank Miller, I will never forgive you, if you or the boys don't come back. I will always love you. But I will never forgive you." Her words were unmistakable in the truth they held.

They all paused their discussion. Those were powerful words. They all knew she had meant them.

"Pops, we're going with you." Ben had yielded to David, eighteen minutes his senior. They all knew what their father had decided, despite his protestations.

When Hank didn't immediately answer, David resumed, "Pops, we can't let you go on your own. We couldn't trust you to look after yourself on your lonesome."

"I can't put you boys in danger. I've survived too many deadly encounters. I know what they are like. Telling the tales as I did when you were children made them sound like grand adventures. I have to admit I embellished a bit. They were bedtime stories, nothing more. What they really were in truth were desperate and dirty. They were not fun at the time they were happening. Adventure is a term to use after you survive it. Besides, I don't know if my luck will rub off on you. Or even if mine has plumb run out." Hank sometimes lapsed into his colorful drawl in times of stress. This was that sort of time.

Heedless of the paternal advice and filled with the sense of immortality of youth, Ben chimed in, "Pops, it's our turn now. Whatever you do, we need to do it together. Finishing college, if need be, can wait. David and I can always catch up. We would feel guilty the rest of our lives if anything happened to you that we might have prevented."

That clinched it. Hank knew a lot about guilt. He didn't want his boys to share the painful lessons he had learned. Then again, he could not bear the guilt, should something happen to them.

They spent the rest of the evening making plans, discarding them, and then starting from scratch. By midnight they all decided to sleep on it and resume the next morning.

It took three days to formulate a blueprint. Hank had been to Morocco before and hoped that experience would help ensure the success of whatever scheme they came up with. They all contributed their ideas, even the disappointed Rachael and the resigned Elizabeth, especially Elizabeth. It was an intricate undertaking, one that required a whole lot of individuals to agree to do their part. And to carry it out. Successfully. If anyone or anything went wrong, they would all be in deep trouble and might not come out of it alive. Hank was relying on some degree of luck, a commodity he worried he had depleted with so many escapes from sure death. A cat might have nine lives. But a Hank might not have nearly that many. He reckoned that he already had used up quite a few.

To start, Hank would send a letter to Colonel Figgins in the London office. It requested that he go to Morocco and contact Jasmina in person to begin the rescue operation. Hank also needed a Maxim gun. Hank made it clear that the mission would be dangerous and would in no way affect the retired colonel's employment. If he failed to agree, they would have to find someone else. But they knew he was the best man for the job. He had trained a goodly portion of the sultan's military and was familiar with the country's language, customs, and geography. And Figgins was the one person they knew who had the connections to procure the Maxim. He was perfect for the job if only he would accept his part in the mission.

***

Colonel Figgins had retired from the military three years before. Despite a distinguished career, he was broke, dead broke with a wife and four children to support. Unfortunately, the gambling bug had bitten an otherwise honorable man.

Hank and Elizabeth first met the colonel immediately after his retirement. He had answered an ad in the *Times of*

London for a manager of their newly opened office. He brought along two letters of reference from actively serving army officers, one a brigadier general. His credentials were impeccable. However, it was his honesty that impressed them. Figgins freely admitted to a gambling problem and the dishonor he felt he had brought on himself. It was a remarkable admission for a proud military man with a distinguished career. The upper crust British accent certainly didn't hurt his effort to attain gainful employment. Americans were always impressed by a well-spoken Brit. Hank and Elizabeth were no exception. Hank recalled a letter from his benefactor, Mr. Hasan Al-Aziz, and a certain Col. Figgins mentioned in it as a reference. He could not help but ask, "Colonel, did you know Mr. Al-Aziz?"

"Yes, of course. Good chap. Passed a year or two ago, I'm afraid. Why do you ask?"

Hank explained. It was a coincidence of Dickensian proportions or a mark of destiny. Either way it was a fateful meeting.

They hired him on the spot. Figgins was forever grateful to them for taking a chance and giving him a loan to restart his life. By then, he had overcome his habit, but had no money to show for it. Now he felt he owed them a debt beyond the repayment he had already made. And he was eager for the chance to have one last adventure in a country he had learned to love. A week later the telegram arrived. It contained one word, "Done." The coded messages he devised would fit his personality. Figgins was a man of few words, at least, most of the time. To maintain secrecy the less said, the better. The first part of their scheme was now set in motion.

Chapter 3:
Laredo, Texas. June 5, 1883

(Twenty-nine Years Earlier or Thereabouts. The Past)

The Gunfight

"I've been hunting you for seven years," Sam Bass spit out. "You kilt my brother, and now it's time to pay."

Hank had wandered aimlessly eastward after leaving El Paso. He had that reward money and was in no hurry to find himself a new profession. He found himself in Laredo one day and decided to take a rest from his travels. He had grown weary of the saddle and wanted to sleep in a real-life bed, at least until he felt it was time to move on.

Hank tried his hand as bartender, store clerk, and bank teller. He quickly tired of them all. He finally hired on as a cowpoke at a ranch a couple of miles outside of town. The boss, Mr. Zebulon Pickett, liked the idea of having what he thought of as a tough guy, good with a gun in his employ. Hank's exploits had followed him to Laredo. Trouble was,

Hank didn't want to be thought of as a gunman. He simply wanted to get on with his life. It was a difficult time for him. He had not yet come to terms with the killing he had done. Yes, those murderers had it coming to them. He had dealt out the justice they deserved. But it never sat right with him, killing that is. Besides, what would happen if he lost his temper like he did when he found Charlie? Would he kill someone in an uncontrollable rage? And he always worried that a friend or relative of those dead men was out for revenge. Best to stay anonymous. What better way to remain that way than to live as a ranch hand out of town?

***

After three years as a wrangler and cowpoke, Hank decided that he had had enough of angry horses wanting to throw you and ornery longhorn cattle wanting to poke you. The dust was enough to choke a mule most days. It didn't matter whether it was summer or winter. The wind always seemed to be in your face, carrying that West Texas dirt into your nose and mouth. It blew right through the kerchiefs most cowboys wore. He was twenty-two or thereabouts and knew it was time to find something new. So, he said his goodbyes to the other hired hands, saving Mr. Pickett for last.

"Son," his boss said, "You are a mighty good worker. I'm sorry to see you go. My advice to you is keep that Colt of yours handy. You'll need it one day." He was right.

Hank rode into town, fixing to get supplies before heading into the sunset or so he believed. Just as it happened in El Paso not that many years ago, fortune or misfortune, depending how you looked at it, shined upon him once again. *Sheriff wanted*, the sign said, posted in a window of Mr. Hatigrove's General Store. Following where fate had led him, he dismounted, tied his horse to the hitching post and went in. Later, in a reflective mood, Hank was never sure why he would have wanted the job. He was young and did it on impulse, he guessed. He had discarded his prior reticence for any high-profile position, especially one in which he might have to use his gun once more.

"Good afternoon Mr. Hatigrove. I saw that sign you have posted in your window. Where should I inquire about it?"

"Well, aren't you a little young for that job? I would have thought you'd have had troubles enough for one lifetime. And that lifetime might not be too long in that particular profession." His notoriety had trailed him right into the general store. Hank had often contemplated changing his name, but felt a mysterious pull to keep it as his own. He never quite understood why he didn't go ahead and purely move to California or anywhere no one knew his reputation.

"What happened to Sheriff Parkhust?"

"Well, he went ahead and packed up one day and took the stage to Fort Worth. You know he was a widower and had no children. Had no real ties to the community. Folks said he was plumb tuckered out of being a lawman. Rumor has it that he bought a store like this one. Gone off to be a shopkeeper, he did. His deputy, Joe Polk, is too old for the job. Barely gets around. That old leg wound of his from the War keeps him from moving as fast as a sheriff needs to."

With the information about Deputy Polk in mind Hank was hopeful that the town would welcome a young man as sheriff.

He repeated his initial query, "Mr. Hatigrove, I was wondering where should I go to inquire about the job?"

"Why at the mayor's office, Hank," shaking his head at the question. He was too polite to say what he was thinking, "Where else would you go?"

"Head on down past Johnson's Saloon. Next door you'll find the mayor's office. Look for the sign saying *Mayor's Office.*"

Hank caught the sarcasm but chose to ignore it. He reckoned it wasn't a real good idea to antagonize a prominent resident of the town. Folks didn't take kindly to young people sassing their elders. All he said was, "Much obliged," and headed out.

When he reached Mayor Root's office, he knocked gently and opened the door. He found him with his feet up on the battered desk, quietly snoring. The aroma of old cigar smoke filled the room. Hank was momentarily baffled. He didn't want to wake the sleeping official and perhaps embarrass him. The young man quietly exited, rapping on the door with a good deal of force this time. He paused before entering. The mayor awoke in a foul mood, having been so abruptly awakened from his afternoon siesta.

"Who is that?" he boomed. "Why do you have to be so dat blamed loud? Couldn't knock politely, couldya?"

Taken aback and fearful of having alienated what he hoped would be his future employer, all Hank could do was stammer, "I'm rightful sorry sir. I did not mean to startle you."

Somewhat mollified, Root continued in a milder tone, "Well come on in, son. I don't like to be disturbed when conducting important city business." He quickly recovered his avuncular self. Afterall, he didn't know if this person standing before him was a potential voter. "What can I do for you?" Like I always ask folks, "What can I do for this here town of ours?"

"Well, sir, I saw that sign over at Mr. Hatigrove's. You know, the one advertising for a sheriff."

"Uh huh."

"I want to apply for the job."

"Aren't you a little young for such a weighty position?"

Hank stood as tall as he could. He was five-foot-seven and change, broad at the shoulders and already mildly bowlegged from so much time spent in the saddle. He had an angular nose and a strong, cleft chin. That latter feature added to his popularity among the women folk. And he had that scar on the left side of his head. It was intriguing to them. His face was handsome in a rough, manly way. He carried himself well, utterly unaware of his effect on those of the opposite sex. In fact, that lack of awareness served to increase his appeal. Unfortunately for him, he had never put those attributes to good use. His appearance, however, didn't help him among men. They measured him by a different standard. They would judge him by how tough they figured he was or how well he could handle a plow or a gun.

"Well, sir, that's a truth, if there ever was one. I've been on my own since I was fifteen. I do have experience as a lawman. A couple of years back I rode shotgun for Wells Fargo." He thought it best to omit from his resume the time he spent rustling cattle.

"Wait, wait. Hold on there. Aren't you that Miller boy? The one that shot dead all those desperados."

Hank knew that fact might come in handy one day. He also worried it might lead to a premature grave. Either way, it dogged him wherever he went.

"Yes, sir, I am."

"Well, what do you know about keeping the peace? It looks like all you know is how to disturb it."

Hank stood up straight and responded with as much bravado as he could muster, "I am a fast learner, sir. I've learned the trade of barkeep and bank clerk and cowhand. I am a first rate shot. I can outrun and outride most men. It was Charlie Breen himself who taught me the importance of upholding the law and following the rules."

Root didn't know who Charlie Breen was, but it sounded impressive. "That's a heap a do'ins for one as young as you. Is that all true?"

"Yes sir, it is. Old Charlie told me not to lie."

That last one didn't impress so much, knowing the ins and outs of politics as he did. In spite of his initial misgivings, the mayor acquiesced, "Okay Hank Miller, I'll give you the job. But on a trial basis. Go on down to the sheriff's office and tell Joe Polk you're to be the new sheriff. Bring back the tin star, and I'll rustle up Judge Cleary to have you sworn in."

That was the beginning of Hank's new career as a lawman. It would last several years, until the hankering for the sunset hit him again.

***

"I've been hunting you for seven years," Sam Bass spat out, "You kilt my brother, and now it's time to pay."

Hank had taken the job as sheriff one year before. The newly minted lawman now faced a deadly killer. The gunslinger's words rattled around in Hank's head as he lounged in the chair outside his office like he'd seen Sheriff Coke do when he brought in those dead men. It was a hot and dry morning that fateful day in the year of our Lord, June fifth, 1883. His past had come a-calling.

"I don't believe we've met." Calm as a purring kitten he was. "I don't set store in violence. Why on earth would you want to kill me? You're bound to die. Either I'll do the job or a noose will."

"I don't much care for your pride, boy. I've tracked you all over this accursed state. Now you stand to die for killing my brother Joe. I'm Sam Bass, and I am the last thing you will see on this earth before I send you to hell."

"Well, this is the fearsome Sam Bass. He does look mighty fearsome, and I sure am afeard," Hank mused. He didn't let it show. Instead he said, "I once vowed to myself never to run from a fight, and I aim to keep that promise."

In his year as sheriff, he had never crossed paths with a real gunslinger before, at least as best he could recollect. This one looked the part. Holster slung low, tied down just right. Fancy shirt, buttoned to the neck. Brown-striped, grey pants. His boots were a little too dusty though. No shine to them at all.

"Well Mr. Bass," he said, smooth as the silk vest that the gunman wore, "We don't cotton to shoot outs in this town.

Not since I became sheriff. I don't know what I can say that will dissuade you from this deadly course you seem so bent upon."

"You can say sorry and then die. If you don't stop jabbering and get yourself out of that chair right now, I'm going to shoot you where you sit." He was getting riled, mighty riled.

Hank knew that a gunfight was inevitable and wanted Bass as agitated as he could make him. The Ake brothers had taught him that the angrier an adversary, the more likely he was to make mistakes. He remembered his own lapse in judgement when rushing to chase down that wounded murderer in the dark. He wasn't going to repeat that same misstep. Hank took his time getting up from the chair, never taking his eyes off the gunman's right hand. His movements were languid, a strange calm coming over him. His focus narrowed, his attention on one thing only, the man opposite him who wanted to kill him. He kept his left hand in his pocket, holding Charlie's old locket with the picture of Sue inside.

Hank ambled down the wooden sidewalk and onto the dusty street. "Everyone clear out now. I don't want any innocent bystander accidentally shot by Mr. Bass here." The townsfolk had already edged into doorways and shops. By this time, the two were twenty paces apart.

"You little son of a whore. Those were your last words." In fact, those were Bass's last. He went for his gun, but before he could clear his holster, he was dead, shot clean through the heart. He never even heard the sound of the gun that killed him, collapsing backward from the impact.

Hank stood there numbly, staring at the dead man lying on the ground, blood beginning to pool beneath him. He still had the Colt in his hand. Mayor Root was the first to come up to him. Everyone else seemed too stunned to move. "That was the darndest thing I ever saw. I barely saw your hand move. You must be the fastest gun there ever was."

Hank holstered his pistol. All he said was, "I was lucky I guess. I always been lucky."

Chapter 4:
Nob Hill, San Francisco. December 11, 1893

(Nineteen Years Earlier or Thereabouts. The Past)

Obsessions

T his here is my second try at an essay as Beth calls them. She said she liked that first one while she diplomatically corrected my grammar. I try to use new words in each of my compositions (That's another one I hadn't tried on before, *composition*. It feels uncomfortable, like a stiff pair of trousers worn for the first time.) I chose another, *diplomatically*, instead of *gently*, a word I had used many times, mostly to describe how my wife treated the children and me.

Tonight I finished reading *Moby Dick*, one of the many books my wife assigned to me. I confess I don't rightly remember ever thinking about whales when out there on the Texas plains. And I never came across anyone called Ishmael. Call me anything you want, but don't call me Ishmael (I put that funny in for you, Beth.)

Beth has instructed me to read a frightful passel of books. I'll get through them all right. I aim to catch up on all the educating I missed as a boy, with Beth's help, of course. I admit it's difficult running a business by day and reading by night. But I never needed much sleep. Four or five hours and I'm ready to go. Keeping the light on in bed at night doesn't seem to bother Beth none. She starts reading her own book and drifts off after an hour or two. She seems to sleep a lot, now that she is with child. I don't rightly know how she does it. All that work at the office, tutoring me at home. Thank goodness for Annie, our cook and housekeeper.

Before I go on any further, I feel I ought to list the other works that Beth has laid down as a foundation (I looked that word up, too. This one felt comfortable like old slippers.), the building books of my education.

The Mayor of Casterbridge
The Last of the Mohicans
Les Miserables
A Tale of Two Cities
Great Expectations
The Scarlet letter
Walden, or A Life in the Woods
Leaves of Grass
Poems by Emily Dickinson

Beth said after I finish those, we'll start on Shakespeare. I recall a play we read in the James School for Boys. I was thirteen or fourteen. It was called *Romeo and Juliet.* I do see a likeness between their romance and ours. We sure seem to have fractured into warring clans, the Franklins on one side and this lone Miller on the other. Blessedly, our romance had a better outcome.

Well, back to old Moby. Mr. Melville got me thinking about obsession. When does taking a keen interest in a thing cross over to obsession? Is there a well-marked border somewhere in the mind that separates the two? Is there someone up there in the brain that guards a gate, like some kind of customs official? Or is it like the Rio Grande, meandering along, sometimes in Mexico and sometimes in the US?

Old Sam Bass had an obsession: killing me because I had done the very same to his brother, even though I was justified in my actions. I handed out justice. He wanted to hand out vengeance. He had spent seven years tracking me … in between shooting other folks, that is. Bass had chased me far and wide, as they say. Not as far as Captain Ahab chasing that white whale of his, but far enough.

I admit that I took great care after that gunfight with him. You might say I was obsessed with my own safety. By then we had all heard about Mr. Hitchcock's dead man's hand, aces and eights. I resolved never to sit with my back or my front to the door in any establishment. After all, you could get yourself shot in the front almost as easily as in the back. And it didn't have to happen in a saloon. So, I always sat off to the side where I could keep my eyes on all the comings and goings. As sheriff, I kept to the shadows during my evening rounds of the town. This was tiring work, this was, having to keep constant vigilance. Constant worry can wear a man down. I convinced the mayor who, in turn, got the town council to hire another deputy to watch my back.

And I always carried Charlie's locket with me in the left pocket of my trousers (I am right-handed and need to keep that hand free to get to my gun.) It wasn't that I was superstitious. I just saw no need to tamper with my luck. Well, I admit maybe this also was a kind of obsession. Most important, it was a way of always remembering Charlie and his lessons to be presentable and follow the rules.

I ask myself then, is an obsession always bad? Some would say Mr. Edison is obsessed with inventing things. He went through ten thousand tries till he finally got the light bulb he wanted, didn't he? (The inventor was once supposedly queried by a reporter, "How did it feel to fail ten thousand times?" He is said to have responded, "I didn't fail ten thousand times. I just found ten thousand ways it didn't work.") That's certainly a positive way of looking at things, isn't it? Was that persistence or obsession? Is there an absolute difference between the two? Is one better than the other? Do we decide based on the success or failure of an endeavor? It seems to depend on one's perspective. And mine is ever changing.

No one would argue that chasing after a huge, murderous whale is a real great idea, would they? I don't think most folks would call Ahab persistent. They would say he was obsessed. But is it a bad thing to render moral judgement about that chase? I ask myself whether an obsession is ever immoral or ever moral? Does good or bad even apply?

Chapter 5:
New York City. July 2, 1912

(The Present)

The Mission Begins

Part One—Business Travel

Beth and Hank spent almost three months of every year visiting their offices in Chicago, New York, and London. Afterall, they had an empire to oversee. They took their children, once of an age able to travel. Anna, their faithful cook, housekeeper, and nanny, would accompany them until the children no longer needed close tending.

They would arrange their trips to coincide with what they thought was the best time of year to visit. They had studied the history and demographics of each city before establishing an office there. Partners in life and business, they knew it was critical to understand potential clientele. Their first stop was always Chicago in late spring (never,

ever in the winter. Beth and Hank had learned that lesson all too well.) They regretted missing the World's Columbian Exposition of 1893. That fair had been an architectural and technological marvel. What a wonder Mr. Ferris's giant Wheel must have been. The passenger conveyances that circled it were the size of railway cars. Unfortunately for them, it had been dismantled before they opened their branch there. They knew that most civic-minded Chicagoans chafed under its sobriquet as America's Second City, the first of course, being New York. That White City, as the exposition was called, and the permanent massive structures that would eventually line the river which flowed through town, were an attempt to become first among America's municipalities. Chicago never smoked that cigar. It had come close.

The next stop was always Philadelphia, home of the Franklins, Beth's parents. It was an awkward time for all of them. The Franklins had never truly accepted Hank, regarding him as a kind of uncultured savage from the frontier. They did have some cause to think that way, at least at first. His speech was pure backwater, exaggerated during tours to lend authenticity to the stories he told. And his clothing matched the cowboy image he wanted to project. Call him what you will, but Hank was a shrewd businessman from the outset. He had lived a rough and ready life that he drew upon for his tours. There was more to him, however, a sophistication he took great pains to hide.

Beth had long ago grown tired of defending her husband. She visited her parents out of filial duty, hoping one day that they would acknowledge her husband's worth. The fact that Hank had saved all their lives made no difference to them.

Their annual pilgrimage to Nob Hill to visit their daughter and grandchildren was a stilted affair. Well, that's not entirely correct. They did show affection for four of the five members of the household. Her parents credited their daughter, not their son-in-law, with how the children had turned out. Hank tolerated the insults, ostensibly ignoring the inevitable, dismissive comments that burned his hide. When it came to Hank, the elder Franklins were masters of casual cruelty. On a few occasions he even fingered Charlie's locket, always in his left pocket. He had trained himself to remain calm in dangerous circumstances, like the Ake brothers had taught him. And that Philadelphia duo could surely create dangerous circumstances. He always managed to control himself. Sometimes, though, it was a close thing.

After the family visit, Beth and Hank would continue their journey east by train to New York, always in the fall to take advantage of the seasonal change in foliage. They never ceased to marvel at the spectacular multicolored displays they felt nature had reserved solely for them. The pair, always together, would greet their office staff as they had in Chicago and let the auditors do their work. They would take the time to meet with their employees to make sure things were running smoothly. Beth, in particular, took the time to listen to their concerns and suggestions. She would implement the best ideas. It made for a happy staff and a happy staff was good for business. What also made their employees happy was the salary, well above what they could make working for competitors or most anyone else. The two of them could afford to pay well to hire and retain good people. Their touring enterprise was wildly successful. But they had another source of wealth, one that no one outside the immediate family knew about, not even her parents.

They would always reserve enough leisure time to take boat excursions up the Hudson or the train to Saratoga Springs to take in the races, the incredible displays of foliage, and the ostensibly health-inducing mineral waters. Neither really liked the salty, rusty taste of those springs after the first sample. The children nearly spit it out on the first try. A stern "Don't you dare" halted what would have been an embarrassing spectacle.

In the evenings there was the theater, perhaps, the most vibrant in the world, London notwithstanding. By the turn of the century Beth and Hank had studied all of Shakespeare together in nightly sessions after dinner. One of his plays or another was always to be found somewhere in town. The performances brought to life the written word.

And there was the Metropolitan Opera and the shows on Broadway. The Met and the Zeigfield Follies were reserved for the adults, the former too boring for the children, and the latter too stimulating. They had to admit New York was their favorite city, outside of San Francisco, that is. They had often toyed with the idea of building a second home there. Beth and Hank favored the area around Central Park. They would often spend their leisure time strolling through its many paths, particularly enjoying the lush and colorful vegetation. It was remarkably different from the flora native to northern California.

The two of them well knew that the population of nearly five million had tripled from the time they had first set up their office in 1896. It was Manhattan in particular that was a great pool of wealth from which to draw tourists out West and later to the European excursions. The two of them studied the rhythms of the city. They learned how to advertise and compete in a uniquely American urban environment. They enjoyed the hustle and bustle of what was rapidly becoming the world's financial and cultural center. Londoners and Parisians would dispute that, of course, but in private recognized the sea change in power that was occurring across the Atlantic. New York grew tall, very tall and Chicago grew wide, very wide. However, Hank had to admit that the brusqueness of New Yorkers rankled him. No one out West would behave that way. At least most folks wouldn't. You might have even come across a polite outlaw or two in Texas.

Then it was on to London, first by a White Star liner and later by their own ship, *The Beth*. After concluding their business there, they never missed the opportunity to visit Paris, the most beautiful city they had ever seen. The Ritz was a magnificent place to stay. Even the St. Regis in New York could not compare. However, no matter where they traveled, they carried San Francisco in their hearts.

Part Two—The Mission

They were in motion as soon as the telegram from Col. Figgins arrived on the twenty-ninth of June at the office in San Francisco. "Done," was all it said. It was the prearranged code that contact had been made with Jasmina. She had agreed to participate. Like the other members of the rescue party, she had a debt to pay. What better way to do so than to free a brave man and her innocent daughter?

Jasmina was the youngest daughter of the now deceased Hasan Al-Aziz and half-sister to Ahmed, the one who inherited his father's position and the bulk of his fortune. The one who had impoverished Ali in revenge for being the recipient of his father's affection. The one who was now responsible for placing Hank and his sons in immeasurable danger. He had let his jealousy of his father's general overcome what little decency he possessed.

Now married to the leader of a rival clan, Jasmina would honor the debt she owed to both Ali and Hank. Her husband was only too eager to allow her to enlist in the rescue. Although allied by marriage, he despised Ahmed, regarding him as a poor successor to his esteemed father. He had appropriated the title of pasha for himself. Neither Sultan Abd al-Aziz ben Hassan, nor his successor Sultan Abd al-Hafid ben Hassan had bestowed that honor on him. Little did she know that her half brother hungered for the sultanate itself. If he were to ascend to the throne, the entire country would suffer. Greedy for power and hungry for the prestige that eluded him, Ahmed had alienated the other tribes in the mysterious region called the Rif, and beyond. But he was clever and ruthless, a foe not to be underestimated. And he possessed great wealth.

Using his contacts, Figgins had been able to gain an audience with Jasmina at her estate outside of Tangier where she spent her summers. There he explained the plot. The first step was to have one of her trusted servants travel to Ahmed's fortress in Zinat, posing as a rice merchant. He would verify that Ali was still alive and, if so, deliver a cryptic message of hope to him. The words to be spoken were, "Letter received.

On way." Nothing was to be in writing. If intercepted, the servant would have no idea what those words meant. Next, she needed to set the bait. Jasmina was to send a letter to her half-brother on behalf of both Hank and a renegade former British officer previously stationed in Morocco, offering a Maxim gun in exchange for Ali and his daughter. Ahmed would know why that debt needed to be paid. Hank felt he owed Ali his life. He would supply whatever it cost to pay the bribes to secure the weapon. The Brit would have the contacts to get hold of it. He would pretend that he wanted to be paid for his efforts, hence the demand for ten thousand British pounds. Hank thought that the insistence on payment was a nice touch, the greed just enough to make the offer seem even more credible. It was Figgins' idea. They all hoped that the lure of the machine gun would be irresistible to a man obsessed with achieving dominance over his rivals. That weapon would surely supply the means. Figgins and Hank would make the delivery in person. Ahmed readily accepted. The delivery date was set as between July twenty-fourth and thirtieth, the seven-day spread to account for the vagaries of travel across the ocean and a relatively perilous landscape in Morocco.

Jasmina's husband, through emissaries, made the necessary bribes to the Berber tribes through whose territory they would pass. His name carried great weight with them. Nevertheless, the pasha's reputation and gold were not a guarantee of safe passage. Rogue elements still might see Hank's party as a target too tempting to pass up.

***

Hank had begun his first trip to Morocco with great anticipation. He had begun this one with a great sense of dread. The three men traveled by trains to New York City, arriving at the newly constructed Penn Station. They went straight to Beth's favorite place to stay in the city that was second in her heart.

They quickly installed themselves in a suite at the St. Regis. The Miller family was well known to the staff from their yearly two-week visits. Their company had often booked out of town guests as a stopover while waiting for *The Beth* to steam them to Liverpool or Marseilles. They knew its history, having endured the latest tutorial offered by the obsequious general manager. The hotel was a monument to luxury built by John Jacob Astor IV. Astor was one of the richest men in the world when he died earlier that year aboard the *Titanic*. His pregnant second wife, Madelaine, survived. He had convinced her to board a lifeboat without him, reportedly telling her, "The sea is calm. You'll be all right. You're in good hands. I'll see you in the morning." Hank hoped for better luck.

Hank had arranged for passage to England on his own liner. It was to be a last-minute departure with few other guests. *The Beth* was a small ship as passenger liners of the day went. The *Titanic* dwarfed her. Thankfully, she was made of sturdier stuff, having made the crossing more than two dozen times without incident. After the tourists disembarked in Liverpool, they would take on supplies and the Maxim before sailing on to Tangier.

He never informed the captain or the crew the true reason for the journey, telling them that he and his sons were off to Morocco to establish a new office for future tours. It was necessary to help keep their operation secret. The deception would also safeguard the crew. In case of discovery they could truthfully deny any and all knowledge of the owner's intent.

In point of fact Hank did not really believe that the crew would be in any serious jeopardy. Nonetheless, honest that he was, he did let them know the voyage might be a tad risky. He offered the captain an extra seven thousand dollars, the other officers four and the rest of the crew two. These were enormous sums for the time. For the sailors princely was the word that came to mind. Hank and Beth had always treated them well. They had built up a bank of trust and good will over the years. Thus, in spite of the word that Hank had used, "risky," they all signed on. And there was nothing like a large paycheck to overcome any misgiving.

The tricky part was to get the Maxim aboard. That machine gun was a fearsome weapon. That was why they chose it as bait. It was Ben who had come up with the idea. He had completed a course in British military history the previous semester at Harvard. He had taken pains to explain to the rest of his family that the weapon was a major technological advance over its hand cranked predecessors like the Gatling gun. A water-cooled wonder, as he described it, the device utilized its own considerable recoil to continuously load ammunition. The British had employed it to great effect in creating and maintaining their empire. Jasmina had dangled it before Ahmed, and he took the bait. They hoped he remained hooked and could reel him in.

Through his network in the military and a few sturdy English pounds, Figgins had managed to have it disappear from the Aldershot Garrison. The inquiry that followed never identified the culprits.

The loading was accomplished in the evening, the Maxim having been packed in a crate marked, *Tomatoes. Fragile. Handle with Care. Keep in Cool Storage.* Somehow the incongruent heaviness of the wooden container ostensibly filled with tomatoes never aroused suspicion. The stevedores either never bothered to question the labels or they thought that rich people must eat really weighty vegetables. Figgins had given the captain specific instructions to keep the tomatoes cool. *The Beth* sailed off two days after it had arrived. Up until now, everything had gone according to plan. Hank broadcast a radio message to the home office in San Francisco: "Off to Tangier." It would be relayed by messenger to Elizabeth and Rachael anxiously waiting for word at home. It was another prearranged code to indicate that all had gone well.

The sailing would take another six or seven days to reach their destination. They trusted that Figgins would meet them at the dock as planned. It had been smooth sailing so far. Little did they anticipate the rough seas that lie ahead.

***

The Colonel was indeed waiting for them at the dock when they arrived. He stood motionless in easily recognizable military bearing. Figgins wore his tan linen suit like a uniform. He waved to the three Americans aboard the ship.

"By all the saints it is a grand thing to see you, Hank. These must be your two sons. Strapping lads they are."

They clasped hands in hearty greeting. Then the colonel heartily clutched the twins' hands.

"Ah, which is Ben and which David?"

As usual they answered in unison. "Ben." "David." They spoke so quickly it was hard to tell who was who. Figgins shook the hand of each young man in turn, the firmness a comforting indication of his strength and character.

"It's all set," he told them. "That grimy bastard Ahmed agreed to the transaction. Bloody hell if I will allow him to ruin the lives of Ali and his daughter. Trained that man myself. Good soldier. Good man."

Hank responded, "Great work Colonel. When do we start?" He always addressed Figgins as Colonel. It was a matter of respect. Hank had always admired members of the military for their service and sacrifice. This was a way of showing it to a man who had found a way to recover his dignity.

"It's Figgins, please. I deserve no more and no less from the person who allowed me to redeem myself to my family. Besides, how else could I possibly continue to call my employer by his first name? I've given up all that formality. By Jove, I have." He failed to mention that he really disliked his given name, Archibald, and that detestable abridged version, Archie. He recalled the distaste he felt when his superior officers would say, "Ah there you are, Archie my good man." Strange the things that bothered one, he thought, and to think of them at a time like this.

Hank agreed to his request, "Well, I guess if it makes you comfortable Colonel, I'll call you whatever you like as long as it isn't Archibald." He had guessed correctly.

The Millers shared a laugh at Figgins' expense. All in good fun, old boy. Losing his customary stoic expression, he actually cringed. It was remarkably expressive for an individual skilled in masking his emotions. He took the kidding well. Figgins knew he was among friends and teasing came along with their friendship. Comrades-in-arms they were. Hank and his boys had kidded one another nearly their entire lives. It was a mark of the confidence they had in each other. Figgins now knew he had truly been welcomed into the Miller family. Besides, Hank had a sense of humor that had dried in the Texas sun and aged well with time. He wanted to pass it along to his children.

Seeing Tangier again triggered memories of an earlier time, twenty-one years before. Hank had surely endured an adventure then. He dwelled on that word, adventure, a thing he had warned his boys about. He feared for them. But he was here to pay a debt and rescue a friend.

And there was the Rif. Even its name conjured visions of ancient mysteries. They would need to cross that region to reach their destination in Zinat. In places, Hank knew, it was ruggedly mountainous and in others a grassy plain. He knew because he had been there before. Above all else, however, he knew it was dangerous.

Figgins had already organized most of the details for passage to the stronghold in Zinat. They could set out in two days. It would take that amount of time to finalize all the other preparations. In the meantime, he offered his services as tour guide in Tangier.

They first checked into the Hotel Continental. To Hank's eye it had little changed since he had last stayed there. Strange how things repeat themselves and how the past, for good or evil, always seems to dog your trail.

***

As their guide, the colonel was uncharacteristically talkative. He was a veritable two-legged travelogue. Listening to Figgins brought their studies to life.

"This is an ancient city by any standard. It was founded by the Phoenicians, you see, sometime between the eighth and tenth centuries B.C. Skip forward a bit now, shall we. A thousand years to be exact." He briefly stopped for effect and then continued, "It was during your George Washington's time that the United States opened a consulate here. They say the city has about forty thousand residents now, not counting the French, of course. Here's the heart of it then.

"By century's end the Frenchies took control of the city. You can see that quite clearly. Everywhere about town they are. About as numerous as frogs at a lily pond. Split the difference with the Spaniards for the rest of the country, they did. Them in the north. Spain in the south. The Kaiser decided he wanted his share too. Almost came to blows with France, he did. Nasty fellow that Kaiser. Hard to believe that man is grandson to Regina Victoria. That bloke is destined to cause a great deal of trouble one day. Come to a bloody bad end, he will. Sooner the better."

Figgins changed to a quiet and furtive tone. "Think it's best if I stop there. Said too much in public already. We don't want to be overheard discussing politics. Compliment one side. Offend another. Never know who's listening. Spies for one side or another everywhere. We can continue later in our hotel rooms. But wouldn't be surprised if someone was listening in there, too. Too many doves flying about."

They had already heard, many times, the ancient proverb that originated from somewhere in this part of the world. The attendant at the front desk, the manager himself who greeted them, the porters all asked the same question. And what brings three Americans to our lovely city? An innocent query now took on sinister overtones. Tangier was a city of international intrigue and foreigners were all suspect. The advice parceled out was always the same, delivered with an index finger over the lips and in conspiratorial fashion, "A secret is like a dove: When it leaves my hand it takes wing." They feared that too many doves had already flown the coop.

The group decided to avoid any further political commentary that might be overheard in public. The last thing they needed was to become embroiled in controversy. They could not afford to draw attention to themselves and have their plot uncovered. Too many people were involved already.

Fortunately, Tangier, city of secrets, was also highly picturesque, one that attracted artists from around the world. It was thus in passing through the Grand Socco Square on their way to the Great Mosque did the four companions happen upon a man dressed in European fashion, carrying a painting. They nodded to each other as they passed. Something caused Hank to stop and ask to see the artist's work. They introduced themselves to one another. Henri Matisse eagerly obliged, unfurling his canvasse of *Window at Tangier*. It was the first time the piece had been on display, so to speak, and a marvelous display it was. The artist was so taken with them that he invited the group to his room at the Grand Hotel Villa de France to see his other works. With time to spare Hank and his party accepted. There they marveled at *View of the Bay* and *Entrance to the Casbah*. What really drew their attention were the studies of *Zohra* for obvious reasons. She was a local prostitute.

They agreed to reconvene for dinner at the hotel's fine restaurant. It was there that Hank commissioned three works. It was an impulsive and strangely optimistic decision. At that moment he did not give thought to his chances of surviving the mission. Later he wondered what a dead man would do with paintings. Perhaps, Beth and Rachael would treasure them as a reminder of him if he never returned. Or perhaps they might not.

***

It was a sixty-seven-mile journey east to Zinat, a relatively short journey but a highly perilous one. They would need to cross the Rif. Hank and Figgins had each done it before, but separately and at different times and under much different circumstances. The terrain was mountainous in places, windswept and hot, extremely hot in others. It was home to green valleys and fertile farmland. And most importantly, it was occupied by nomadic bands, Berbers, as in pirates and brigands. They were an especial danger to outsiders. Traders traveled in armed caravans. Experienced ones made sure to send emissaries ahead to bribe the tribes to let them pass in peace. Local farmers who lived in verdant stretches paid "tribute" to keep raiders away. It worked, usually. They hoped that Jasmina's husband had paid enough to keep them safe.

Hank, David, Ben, and Figgins set out on their fourth day in the country. Hank took his old Henry. He had kept it in meticulous condition from his frontier days, thirty years before. It held an incredible sixteen shots, and in skilled hands its rapid lever action would nearly rival modern semi-automatic competitors. Hank remained attached to it and had taken target practice whenever the opportunity arose. He did replace his ancient six shooter with the semi-automatic Colt Model 1911. He liked its feel. It was balanced enough to be highly accurate at close range. And Hank was possessed of a steady right hand. Its .45 caliber slug was powerful enough to knock a man backwards. He favored it over the German Mauser because, well, the Colt was American made. Figgins had his Lee-Enfield rifle, a staple of the British army at the time, and his Webley Revolver. The two boys favored the Model 1903 Springfield, a semi-automatic, bolt action long gun, which packed a true wallop. In addition, they each carried the same sidearm as their father and were proficient in its use.

A local dealer furnished the horses they rode. They wanted sturdy animals that would withstand the rigors of rough terrain. Contrary to popular lore, Arabians fit the bill—sleek, strong, and fast. Most importantly, the breed possessed sure-footedness and great endurance. It had taken a bit of convincing, but the boys were able to persuade their father to leave his favorite Appaloosa, Charlie II, behind. The trip to Morocco via New York and England would have been too hard on him. They would rely on Col. Figgins to procure the hardiest mounts. He would know the best breed to buy for the journey, and he did not disappoint. They packed their necessities and tents on the mules.

They had disassembled the Maxim themselves at night while on board *The Beth* and distributed the parts among several crates, labeled *Tools*. The ammunition was carefully packed in insulation to prevent overheating. Figgins had even rigged an umbrella-like contraption to keep the sun off those particular crates housing the cartridge belts. Hank regarded that as an unusual way to transport ammunition but brushed the thought aside. The British could be quite peculiar at times. Figgins would have told them if they were transporting nitro, wouldn't he? Maybe Maxim bullets were sensitive to heat. They loaded crates two per mule directly from the ship, having left them in the care of the captain and crew when they went to their hotel.

Figgins had personally overseen the outfitting as well as the hiring of the mule drivers, cook, and guides. The latter was a father and son duo. He knew them personally while stationed in the country years before. He judged them trustworthy and reliable. They would need to be. All their lives depended on it.

Off they went, hopeful of a smooth journey, but prepared for a rocky one. The telegram to home read, "Z." The women would know they were now on their way to Zinat.

The four of them never lost focus on their mission to save Ali and his daughter. And Hank never forgot a debt. He meant to repay it. There were many creditors to satisfy, even though none of them had ever demanded payment. Hank, Jasmina, and Figgins, each in their own way, felt they owed one another and had to honor their obligations.

Chapter 6:
San Antonio, Texas. April 10, 1887

(Twenty-five Years Earlier or Thereabouts. The Past)

Tours

T he wanderlust hadn't hit Hank for a while. He had been sheriff of Laredo for nigh on five years. He was twenty-eight and had settled into a comfortable routine. He even had himself a girlfriend, Hattie MacDonald. When she suddenly broke off their relationship to go off and marry one of his deputies, it struck hard. That sunset again looked like a mighty fine draw.

Truth be told, he was tiring of being a lawman. It was a dangerous occupation. Hank had become bored arresting the unruly, drunken cowboys who came to town from local ranches to celebrate payday. They were good kids, most of them, except when filled with cheap liquor from the saloons they frequented. Maybe he recognized part of himself in them and didn't like what he saw. Besides, the population had swelled to almost four thousand. It was getting more than he and two deputies could handle. The town council was not yet inclined to hire another deputy or establish a professional police force, the way many large cities had. They had spent so much of their funds building a courthouse and city hall that the coffers were bare. He also feared another encounter with some other vengeful relative of the bushwhackers he had shot years earlier. Fortunately, none had materialized. He wanted nothing further to do with killing. He didn't want to shoot anyone, and he sure didn't want to get shot.

So it was that he came across a full-page ad in a month-old *Dallas Daily Herald*. A company called *International Express Tours* was looking to hire guides for its new Texas branch. The pay was one hundred twenty dollars a month with free room and board. It seemed like an attractive offer. They promised tourists "An adventure of a lifetime in the Wild West under the guidance of real cowboys. Safety and comfort assured." Inquiries were to be sent to an address in New York City. Hank got to thinking, "Why, I know West Texas and the Hill Country like the back of my hand. This tour guide business seems like a safe profession." He turned out to be wrong about that.

Texas was a land of opportunity after the Civil War for those willing and able to grab it. To understand the enterprising mind set you had to grasp the enormity of the state. It was big, real big. You had to think just as big to get ahead. Before the war that very size had limited economic growth. It took near on forever to go from humid Galveston on the eastern coast through the picturesque Hill Country of San Antonio, to Austin the capital, and on to the dry heat of El Paso. The journey from Houston south to Brownsville was an equally arduous one. Those distances impeded commerce. However, after the great conflict, entrepreneurs began constructing railroads throughout the state. These networks provided rapid links among the towns and cities that had been relatively isolated until then. In fact, those very same rails would join others throughout the nation. Some would argue that the iron horse helped to reintegrate the state into the union. Travel powered by horse or mule had been too slow and had kept the state relatively isolated. Others would argue the point, noting that Texas always considered itself too big to be a part of anything. It had been its own country once and had never fully given up the notion.

Hank sensed the change in the business climate. He read the papers from Houston and Dallas that Mr. Hatigrove sold in his store. They might be a week or two late, but that did not alter the news that the winds of change were in the air. Inertia had kept him in Laredo. He had gotten used to a comfortable routine, that is, until a woman's change of heart set those winds of change rushing upon him.

Thought hard about that job in Dallas, Hank did. He didn't want to work for someone else anymore. He had done that all his life. Right then and there he decided his time in Laredo had come to an end. He would start his own firm. The name came to him instantly, *The American West Tour Company*. It was a fateful decision. Little did he know at the time how wildly successful it would become or the extraordinary peril it would put him in.

Hank had kept the reward money from turning in those murderous bandits stashed in the Wells Fargo Bank in town. He led a frugal life, saving much of his salary over the years. He had intended to use his nest egg to buy a home for him and Hattie. Now he would put it toward a different purpose. Hank thought a lot about what he would need to start the venture. He first had the idea of contacting the folks at *International Express*, but quickly discarded it. Why would they want to help a rival get started? He had no experience in running a business. Where could he find the information he needed? Laredo had no public library. He would have to seek advice from any of the townsfolk who operated a successful enterprise.

Mr. Hatigrove was standing behind the counter of his General Store when Hank entered. "What can I do you for, Sheriff?" Their relationship had changed during Hank's tenure in Laredo. He was no longer the rawboned kid seeking employment as sheriff. He was the experienced lawman who kept peaceable order and commanded the respect of the populace, well, most of it anyway. A few of the rowdies he sometimes had to manhandle kept grudges, they did. They never sought revenge, because Hank also inspired fear. His gunfight with Sam Bass had become something of a legend. No one wanted to call him out. Young bucks wanting to make a name for themselves by killing a famous gunfighter were few and far between. Those who worked up the courage to provoke a gunfight were usually besotted with alcohol and didn't survive the day. Prudence overcame ambition for most everyone else.

"Well, Mr. Hatigrove, I come for some advice."

"Ah, Mr. Sheriff, you've come to the right place." The proprietor kept his disappointment to himself. He had hoped that Hank wanted to buy something, preferably something expensive.

"Mr. Hatigrove, I want to start a business of my own."

"Well, I hope it's not a general store you want to open," the older man said with a smile while in the back of his mind he was a-might worried. He already had a competitor who had opened a giant warehouse full of cheap goods. It was stealing his customers at a frightening pace.

"No, no, not that. I want to open a tour company. You know, take folks from back East out on the trail. Put on a right entertaining show for them."

With a measure of relief the proprietor told him, "Why Hank, I run a store, not a tour company. I have no good advice to give you." After a moment's contemplation, however, he figured he did have some advice. "Wait, I do have an idea. Mr. Gregg has a private library all of his own. He owns two saloons and one of the horse stables. Does right well for himself. Why don't you go on over to the *Cowboy's Fancy* and speak with him?"

"Much obliged, Mr. Hatigrove. I think I'll head on over there."

That's exactly what he did. Hank headed down the dusty street, heedless of the riders and buckboards. He was distracted by thoughts of a new life. No harm came to him. Folks found a way of avoiding a collision with a sheriff who seemed oddly contemplative, wandering as he was in the middle of a busy roadway. He thus reached *Cowboy's Fancy* in safety. He peered in first, as he always did, having recovered his sense of caution. He saw no threat and passed through the swinging half doors. The saloon was quiet. It was mid-afternoon, too early for a raucous crowd to gather. One man stood at the bar to the right, nursing a beer. Gregg was sitting alone at a table off to the left on the far side of the main floor. He was dressed in a fine striped woolen suit, shirt with ruffled sleeves topped by a fanciful ascot. He was engaged in squaring accounts in an oversized ledger. He likely lived by Hank's principle to never sit directly in front of an entrance. Hank wondered if he had enemies. He gave that thought a passing glance and walked over to the table.

Gregg halted his work and looked up as Hank approached. "Sheriff, welcome. We don't often see you this time of day. Take a seat. How about a whiskey? Only the best for you."

"No thanks, Mr. Gregg, I do appreciate the offer." Hank was polite when dealing with the citizenry. It was among many things Charlie had taught him so long ago. He had learned he could defuse most tense situations with a dollop of charm and humor. It paid to be polite and had become part of his nature. "I've come to ask a favor."

"Anything for our favorite sheriff. What is it we can offer in the way of wisdom?" Gregg had a way of putting things in a way that often rankled Hank. That use of the royal *we* and *our* in place of *I* and *my* always seemed pretentious.

He quickly put those irritations aside and went on. "I figure on opening my own tour company. I aim to put on a real good show for folks back East who want to experience what they think of as the wild West. Those dime store novels sure seem to have stoked a brisk trade in this business. I need to learn how to get started. I was hoping you would be the person to help point me in the right direction, being the successful businessman you are." A little compliment dropped here and there never hurt. Hank had learned how to read people and instinctively knew who to trust and who not. It was part of the trade of being a good lawman and helped keep him alive. It was a talent that would serve him well for the rest of his life.

Sensing an opportunity, Gregg offered, "If it's money you need, we could stake you a start in return for a part of the business. We'd want to learn about your plans first."

There was that *we* again. Hank controlled his annoyance, "That's a mighty kind offer. It's not money I need. It's information."

It was how Hank then found himself in Gregg's upstairs library. He had never seen anything remotely to compare with this handsome collection before, row upon row of books lining the shelves from floor to ceiling.

"It's a passion of ours, Hank. Reading that is. We love to collect books. This is our fiction collection, pointing to a whole wall near the window. Dickens is my favorite author."

Hank didn't know who Dickens was but was willing to play along. He had a goal in mind and did not want to appear unlettered. He kept silent waiting for Gregg to continue.

"Ah, here it is. Exactly what the doctor ordered, as they say. Stratford's *How to Succeed in Business*. It's yours Hank. My gift."

"Why that's mighty kind of you. I would be happy to pay for it."

"We won't hear of it. It's a gift. Never look a gift horse in the mouth, we say. Go on, Hank. We've read it many times. The paper's worn thin."

And so began a new phase in Hank's life, one of an entrepreneur.

He took the next three weeks studying the text. Hank formulated a business plan. He would start off by mapping out a safe trail to take his guests on. Hank figured he would need a covered wagon to carry supplies and horses. Two to pull the wagon. Not oxen or mules. They weren't a pretty enough sight and would likely disappoint his guests. He favored Morgans for their strength to haul the wagon and Appaloosas for their gentle nature, perfect for Easterners to ride. Hank was a natural entertainer, always attentive to his audience. He had attended Bill Cody's Wild West show six months earlier, which didn't hurt his sense of showmanship either. It was entertainment his guests were after, an immersive experience like none other. He aimed to provide it.

Hank planned on hiring characters for his show. He would also need a good cook. He knew of one who came to town near every three months after each cattle drive. It turned out that "Edgy" Lamont no longer wanted to tolerate the dust and heat and rain and above all else, the constant scent of cow droppings on the open range. He did not have the money to open his own restaurant. But he sure could cook up a meal. His *fixins* were a real draw to cowhands looking for a cattle drive to sign onto. The trail bosses liked having him. Cowpokes called him Edgy because he sure became irritable if they came a-sniffin'after his food before it was ready. No one knew his real first name. So, Edgy it was.

He was easy to recruit. And it turned out he knew a cowhand who might be interested in playing another role Hank had in mind. Tom Breakwater fit the bill, a grizzled veteran of the plains. Punching cattle for near on a dozen years had worn thin on him, and he did not want to miss out when opportunity knocked. He figured he could find part-time work in San Antonio in between excursions. Like his boss, he too was ready for something new.

Hank took the International and Great Northern train from Laredo to what he anticipated would be his new home in San Antonio. He would need a place to live and an office for work. He found both on his second day in town. It was a fine brick building, two stories tall, and located in what was shortly to be called Old Town. He would live upstairs and work on the first floor. Hank then hunted down a boarding house for his employees, negotiating a volume discount on the monthly payment. Details, being thorough, were important to him. He had learned that from the business text. It could mean the difference between success and failure.

It took two weeks to set up the office. By this time he had used up a chunk of his savings. He still had enough to get by, but barely. Taking a lesson from the *International Express Tours*, he took out ads in newspapers in the major cities of the East and as far west as Chicago and St. Louis.

Hank had chosen San Antonio because of its pleasant climate, picturesque river, and relatively gentle terrain. The area that surrounded the city offered beautiful scenery, from desert to verdant hills to forest and waterways. It was perfect for a three or four day excursion. Almost exclusively known to the country outside of Texas as the site of the Alamo, San

Antonio was more than its famous landmark. It was a progressive, thriving city with much to offer. The rest of the country should know that. It became his mission. He eventually accomplished that mission and did it with a flair all his own.

But there was another reason he had chosen San Antonio. He had come home.

Chapter 7:
Nob Hill, San Francisco. August 12, 1898

(Fourteen Years Earlier or Thereabouts. The Past)

Shame

M ark Twain was right. Summers here are mighty cold. I could not resist writing down that observation in this chilly month of August. That remark, however, has no relation to the subject of today's essay.

I finished James Fenimore Cooper's *The Last of the Mohicans* this morning. I had stayed up all night reading. The novel was so exciting I couldn't put it down. One thing still stings, even with what most would consider a happy ending. I feel a measure of the pain I imagined that Chingachgook must have experienced at the loss of his son. It made me think of what it would be like if I were to survive the loss of Ben, David, Rachael or my beloved Beth. How on earth would I be able to go on? I prayed that would never happen. Like most parents, I hope my kids grow up smart and strong;

strong, that is, in both body and mind. I wish them a long and happy life.

Thinking of the children, I remembered Mr. Twain's famous quote, "When I was a boy of fourteen, my father was so ignorant I could hardly stand to have the old man around. But when I got to be twenty-one, I was astonished at how much the old man had learned in seven years." I trust my kids will come to the same conclusion, hopefully, several years earlier. The humor helped me escape the brooding I had fallen into.

And then I thought about names, the names of my children and the people I knew. Natty Bumppo seemed an odd choice of name for the main character. Was it a common one for the time? Come to think of it, I have never come across a Bumppo or a Natty. Family names do die out through marriage and death. Trends in naming babies are subject to change. Take my name, my birth name, for example: Heinrich Samuel Müeller.

I always liked to say that I was born east of the Pecos and west of the Brazos. It wasn't true. I was actually born on a farm north of San Antonio, sometime in 1859 or 1860. I never found out my exact birth date. My father would never tell me. I reckon it was because it was the very same day my mother died, giving life to me. Looking back, it was pretty clear he never recovered from that blow. My father never spoke much. He sent me off to boarding school when I was about six. It was 1865. He put me in the wagon one day and headed out to the Edgar James School for Boys. "I'll see you at Christmas," was all he said as he rode off. It must have been in late fall because I recall a cloudy grey sky with a chill in the air. I admit I did not learn much that semester, except to march and play a military drum roll. Strange as it may seem, even at that young age I did participate in an event of historical significance.

The historians I have read peg the last battle of the Civil War to have occurred on May 13, 1866, at a place called Palmito Ranch, near Brownsville, Texas. They are wrong and not for the technical reasons some authors cite. Yes, other rebel departments remained operational after Lee's surrender of the Army of Northern Virginia to Grant on April 9, 1865. Old Joe Johnston hung on to his Army of Tennessee until later that month but fought no major engagements. No matter. Whatever that army did or didn't do happened before the skirmish at Palmito. There were other smaller rebel battalions elsewhere that took their own good time in surrendering, perhaps as late as June of that fateful year. And yes, a few scholars point to a separate country apart from the Confederate States of America, formed of parts of the Mississippi region after Grant took Vicksburg. But none of these armies or countries fought that very last battle. I know. I was there.

It was the nineteenth of June, 1866, outside Castle Hills, when the confederate picket first spotted the approaching Union cavalry. That date would carry significance for other reasons. It was on that very same day one year earlier that Union Army General Gordon Granger had issued General Order No. 3, declaring all slaves in Texas to be free. It would hence be called by many names, including Jubilee Day. And it would be for this that June nineteenth would be remembered, not for all those who needlessly lost their lives at the school.

The local engagement that had occurred there would be lost to history. Mr. James would retell the story every year on the anniversary of the event. I knew it by heart or at least his version of it by time I was ten.

There was a small rebel camp about a half mile from the school. Either they had decided not to surrender or never got word it was time to stop the killing. Mr. James said there were forty-four soldiers defending our little patch of Texas from those invading barbarians from the North. Patriots he called the defenders of Southern honor. Well, those patriots decided to use our school as their fortress. They occupied all the rooms and dormitories, using overturned desks and mattresses to protect the windows. A lone Union man, mounted on his horse and carrying a white flag crossed the grassy plain that separated his encampment from ours. Mr. James had all of the students line up outside the front door. He stood at the head of his young battalion. I was manning my trusty drum, beating away in a marching tune which still echoes somewhere in my brain. As Mr. James told it, the officer, a blue belly as he colorfully described him, demanded surrender from the rebel commander. As a still loyal lieutenant to the Cause that had long been Lost, he refused. He had never received orders to have his troops turn their muskets into plowshares and go home. The Union officer explained that Lee and Johnston had surrendered over a year ago. The confederate would have none of it. It was Yankee lies. General Lee would never give up. This steadfast little garrison would send the boys in blue back to wherever they came from, tails between their legs. They could whip any Union soldiers from now until Sunday. Absorbing the insults, the cavalry officer told them both to release the children before they attacked. Mr. James refused. This was his land and Attila and his hordes were not going to take it away from him. While the parley was going on, I kept on drumming although my arms ached something fierce.

The next thing I heard were three loud booms as the enemy fired warning shots from their cannons. I had never heard anything in my life that compared to those booms, not even the loudest thunder during a Texas sized rainstorm. I panicked and ran. Apparently, the other children stood their ground with Mr. James valiantly standing at the forefront of that miniature brigade of his. It was not until the brave reb lieutenant told them to skedaddle that they did so. Shortly afterwards the Union cannon demolished much of the school and dormitory. Cowards they were, Mr. James would always say. Afraid of a charge, until their enemy had been reduced from afar. The Federals eventually did charge, capturing the surviving confederates. They were a bedraggled sight, I'm told, scrawny with their butternut-colored uniforms sporting so many patches they resembled worn out quilts.

Mr. James leveled the accusation at me, "Coward you are, Heinrich Müeller. I will write to your father. It is by my mercy and that of the Almighty that you will be spared expulsion and perdition." I did not know what expulsion or perdition were, but those words gave a six-year-old even more of a fright than he already was shaking from. I felt ashamed, a right terrible shame. I resolved then and there to never again run from a fight. I never did.

My father arrived one day in response to the headmaster's missive. He had me stand before the whole school or what remained of it to apologize. All I could muster was a mumbled sorry. We found temporary quarters in town to continue the arduous work of a moral education, until the school could be rebuilt. Most importantly, but neatly omitted by Mr. James in his telling, we buried the three children who followed orders and stood their ground a might too long. I'll never know how those Union soldiers felt about what they had done.

I kept the letter **C** buried deep inside my chest, until a year ago when I read *The Scarlet Letter*. Like Hester Prynne, I was branded for my sin. It started me thinking about the past. You can let it haunt you. I surely did. Mr. Hawthorne had set me on the road to forgiveness. That path lasted a full twelve months. One day I finally decided it was time to forgive a six-year-old for a sin he didn't commit.

N.B. Beth told me that she really liked the content of this composition. She said my vocabulary and methods of expression were improving all the time. But she told me it rambled a bit and should have been split into two separate pieces. The ideas did not always flow together. Funny, how it all seemed to fit together in my mind. I'll be mindful of her suggestions in the future.

I never went looking for a fight. But I still kept that promise I made to myself never to run from one. I suppose a remnant of that **C** survived my efforts to excise it.

Chapter 8:
Nob Hill, San Francisco. July 29, 1912

(The Present)

Homefront

T he two women sat on the piano bench in the music room. Each had tried their hand at playing Beethoven's Piano Concertos 0, 1, and 2. It had not gone well. The fault was not with the Steinway. They simply could not concentrate. The men of the household were at risk. Beth and Rachael could do no more than wait. They were not at all good at that.

The order of battle was long ago assigned. The blueprint to which they all had contributed was already set in motion. Only the participants could alter it as the need arose. They felt helpless merely awaiting the brief coded telegrams that would signal whatever stage the men had reached. Men! Always it was the men who took action. Hank and the boys had left the womenfolk behind as good soldiers always did. In some ways it was galling. In others it was painful, almost unbearable.

The two women wanted to do more. They wanted to protect their loved ones. Beth had done it once before and chafed at not having the opportunity to do it again.

Rachael had read and reread the letter her father had left for her. It was by now stained with her tears, the ink running in many places. She had shown it to her mother who broke down reading it. Beth never showed her daughter the contents of the one Hank had given her. And she had not opened the one meant for her boys. It was to be given to them on their return.

"Momma, Can I ask you a question?"

"Of course, sweetheart, anything."

"I've always wondered what attracted you to papa in the first place. You both seem, well, so different."

Little did the two women know that six thousand miles away a similar conversation was taking place.

Beth paused, a pensive look on her face. "You're old enough now to understand. And by the way we are not as different from one another as you might think.

"When I stepped off that train in San Antonio, I saw a handsome man. Not handsome in a conventional sense. Handsome in a manly way. He was not tall, but he had a good pair of shoulders on him. He stood there with a welcoming smile on his face. He had an air of competence. Not arrogance, mind you. Competence. And when he took off that hat of his, I saw that scar on the left side of his head. It reminded me of pictures of European officers with those dueling scars on their cheeks. That scar was," Beth hesitated before continuing as if gathering her thoughts, "intriguing." She smiled.

"It sounds like he made a good first impression."

"Yes, he did. Until he opened his mouth to speak with that awful fake version of Texan. But three days later I knew he was the one. He saved all our lives, Rachael. You know that. We told you and the boys that bedtime story countless times. However, the reality of it was bloody and frightening and dangerous. I had read many tales of the West as a schoolgirl. This was nothing like it. Except one thing. Your father. He was a hero right out of Ned Buntline. Better really. Far better. I knew then." Beth continued with a mischievous smile, "I also knew I would have to teach your father how to speak English."

They both laughed, that is, until Beth and her daughter suddenly hugged one another. "Momma, what are we going to do if they don't come back?"

"What can I say, sweetheart? I believe in your father. If anyone on this earth can pull this off, it is him. He'll do his best to protect the boys and bring them all back alive with Ali and Amina in tow."

"What if this one time his best is not enough?"

No response was necessary. They knew by the last telegram received on July twenty second, "Z," that the expedition was on course and on its way to Zinat. They would not hear from them for the time it would take to return to Tangier.

Beth and Rachael dutifully went to the downtown office each day. They went on weekends. too. They were well aware that their employees knew their jobs. Yet, there was still an entire empire to oversee, stretching from San Francisco to Europe and passing through four cities and an ocean on the way. The decisions to be made, the telephone calls, the cables and correspondence to be sent and answered proved a ready distraction for them both.

Before that letter from Ali arrived over two months ago, they had been making plans for Rachael to stay with her grandparents in Philadelphia while she attended Swarthmore. Given the Franklin's relationship with Hank, it seemed as if they had been charting a military operation. The pair had giggled conspiratorially as they hatched their plot. They hoped to minimize the hostilities between the parties that they knew would still inevitably occur in some way. In fairness to Hank, he had only once lost his temper with them and that was years ago. Her parents were questioning the instructions he was giving them that would ultimately save all their lives. Since then, he had endured their not-so-subtle slights and outright insults for the sake of maintaining family harmony. Beth's parents had never forgiven him for stealing their child and bringing her to an untamed wilderness. Now though, all those thoughts and plans seemed distant and trivial. They measured time as before and after the arrival of Ali's letter. It would only change back to normal when Hank and the boys returned to safety. The two of them never appreciated the value of the mundane aspects of their lives, until now, that is. They wanted those former lives back.

Beth and Rachael had done their part in the planning stage of the mission. No more could be expected of them by anyone, except themselves.

Chapter 9:
San Antonio, Texas. September 2, 1888

(Twenty-four Years Earlier or Thereabouts. The Past)

Reclaiming History

Hank had another reason to return to San Antonio, besides starting a business. He wanted to claim his heritage. Not his land, mind you. His story. Most everyone else he had become acquainted with knew the saga of their kin. It was passed down from one generation to the next. He wanted his own story. Hank started by asking around town for directions to the Müeller farm. No one seemed to have even heard the name. So, he made his way to the Bexar County Recorder's Office. He spent hours there, until finally locating the deed to what used to be the family farm. He rode out there, hoping to find out the history of his family.

When he arrived, a friendly-looking woman stood in the doorway of the farmhouse. "Howdy, Mrs. Yates. My name is

Hank Miller. I was born Heinrich Müeller," which he pro-
nounced in typical West Texan fashion, *Hine rich Müll er.*

"Well, Mr. *Müll er.* How is it you know my name?"

"That is a long story ma'am. I was hoping you would give
me the time to tell it."

"I'm afraid I ain't got a lot to spare. I need to feed the
hogs and set dinner for my husband." She was not so friendly
appearing anymore.

"Well then, I'll condense the tale, ma'am," as polite as a
waiter hoping for a big tip. He went on. "Look over yonder
at Crabb's Hill. Do you see that headstone atop it?"

Mrs. Yates turned and nodded assent.

"My pa is buried up there. I used to live on this farm. I
am searching for my history. I went to the Bexar County
Recorder's Office over there in San Antone and found you
and your husband's name on the deed to this property. I was
hoping you could tell me something about my kin."

Defensive now, Mrs. Yates replied, "We bought this here
property all legal like. I don't know nothing about your pa or
the rest of your family for that matter." Pausing a moment,
she looked pensive and continued, "Wait a minute now," she
said, rubbing her chin. "Old lady Dundee has lived in these
parts for over sixty years. Her husband passed a while back
and her three sons come by regular as clockwork to make
sure she is safe. Independent she is. My husband and me
bring her an apple pie every Sunday after church. If anyone
knows anything about what you're looking for, it would be
her. She lives about a mile-and-a-half down the road to the
north. I'd pay her a call if I was you."

For someone who had no time to talk, thought Hank, that was a mighty lot of words. Always discreet, or almost always so, he kept that thought to himself. All he said was, "Why thank you, ma'am. You've been right kind. Do you mind if I cross your property to visit with my pa?"

She voiced no objection. He tipped his dusty Stetson, lightly spurring his Appaloosa, "Let's go, Charlie," and rode off.

Hank stopped at the bare gravesite on the hill, never dismounting from his horse, "I'm sorry, Papa, for whatever I did to you. I hope you are resting in peace."

He could think of nothing else to say.

Thirty minutes later he arrived at his destination. Mrs. Dundee was tending a small patch of flowers outside her home. The house was a well-kept residence, freshly painted the white of the clouds passing overhead. She was a slip of a woman, barely over five feet, white haired, and wrinkled. She raised her hand to shield her eyes from the sun, high in the west. Before Hank could utter a greeting, the woman welcomed him, "Hi there Heinrich, pronouncing it in the German way. I've been expecting you. Come on in. I expect a cool glass of water would hit the spot right about now."

Stunned, Hank was for one of the few times in his life short for words. Recovering quickly, he eagerly responded, "Well thank you, Mrs. Dundee. I do believe I will take you up on that kind offer."

"Come on in then. And call me Jane. Mrs. Dundee sounds like you are addressing my mother, may she rest in peace."

Right spritely for her age, Hank observed. He wisely kept that observation to himself. He didn't know how she would take the remark.

He dismounted, tied Charlie to the hitching post, and went on in. The entryway was dim, typically constructed to help ward off the withering Texas heat. She led him into the kitchen and motioned for him to sit.

As she served him the water he could not resist asking, "How on earth did you know who I was?"

"I saw you coming a mile away. My eyesight is just fine for an old lady. You are the spitting image of your mother. I would have recognized you anywhere."

He almost choked on that water but managed to keep it to a sputter. "You knew my mother? How? When?" Hope had sprung loose.

"Before I tell you the tale, how about a slice of fresh apple pie. My neighbors brought it over yesterday."

"I would be much obliged, Mrs. Dundee, er, Jane."

She set down the slice of pie in front of him with a fork and napkin and began the story he had wondered about for so long.

"Hank, your mother and I were best friends. Your father was a difficult man. We would visit each other as often as we could. Our chores would keep us away for most of the week. Your pa was choosier about his meals than my Joe, easygoing as he was. Mind you, I always cooked a fine feed for my husband and children. It was that Karl wanted his food just so, like his mother made it in the old country. He could be quite critical, you know. Anna told me these things because she didn't have anyone else to confide in. Your parents led a pretty isolated life, not hard to do in these parts if you don't make the effort to socialize.

"They had emigrated to Texas from what she told me was Posen Province in 1856. A fella called The Kaiser runs it now as a part of Germany. I read that he is a grandson of Victoria, Queen of England. I read a lot out here even in this backcountry. I've got a pretty good memory, too. Always had. Expect I always will. I carry so many people who have passed up there in my brain. It's the only place they reside now. They're comfortable in that brain of mine. At peace. When I die, so could they. A second death, you see, unless I pass down the stories so someone else can carry them. Like I'm doing with you now. The price for you is to keep close what I tell you up there in your brain. It will keep your ma alive as long as you live, and let you pass on that memory to your children."

Hank nodded assent, "I'll do that as best I can, Jane. I'd swear it on the bible if you happen to have one handy. I do admit I have no children as yet. I do aim to, once I find the right girl. Much obliged for the hospitality and the 'tell'in of my ma."

"No need to swear on anything, Hank. I believe you will. And I don't have the bible you would need."

That last remark puzzled him.

Before he could ask what she meant, Jane went on, "There was a wave of migration from Germany to these parts around the time your parents arrived. But they came for a reason a might different than most others. They were a mixed marriage as they say."

Hank had no idea what that meant, but chose not to interrupt. He was too transfixed by the tale Jane was spinning.

"Your father, your pa, was a Lutheran. Your mother was a Jewess. Anna Miriam Bachstaedter. They had met in the city of the same name as the province. Their secret acquaintance bloomed to love as it often does between a man and woman. They eloped to Alsace-Lorraine, a region then under French control so they could be married in a civil ceremony. When they learned of the union, both families disowned them. They knew that would happen and had already planned to flee to America. They both had friends who were going to Texas; so that's where they went. Your parents chose a place where no one would know them. Castle Hills fit the bill, and here they settled.

"I tell you true. I miss your ma terribly hard, even all these years later. Almost as much as I miss my Joe, maybe more. She was a good woman with a kindly heart. But I've got her right up here." She tapped the side of her head.

"We had shared so much of our lives that a part of me died that same day she did. I was there at your birth and your mother's passing. I know that your pa took it hard. He was a quiet man before and proceeded to stop talking almost entirely after her death. I came when I could to help tend to you. Karl was hardly an affectionate parent. I knew that. He blamed you for Anna's death. He sent you away as soon as you reached the age that the local boarding school would allow. You cannot blame yourself for his lack of affection. He was not a cruel man, but twisted so much inside that he couldn't handle your presence. He pushed you away. It was unforgivable. You deserved better.

"Your father arranged for her to be buried at the Mount Sinai Cemetery in Houston in case you feel the need to visit.

"You have the look of a man who has overcome any harshness unfairly meted out to you. You do have sad eyes though. I expect you have seen your share of troubles. But now, it's your turn. Tell me about yourself. Your mother is listening." Jane again tapped her head. "She'd like to know about the man you've grown into."

Hank told his story. He told it true. Jane listened intently throughout the account.

"Why, Hank, you have lived a remarkable life for someone so young. You must be thirty years old by now. It sounds as if you have already crammed a life or two into that body of yours."

"Well," he replied, "I been lucky, I guess. I could have turned to a life of crime or had my life shortened by quite a stretch, if it weren't for friends who set me straight along the way."

"You have grown into a fine man and need to find yourself a fine wife, Hank. You will make a good woman happy. I know it. I wish I had a daughter to marry you off to. The world needs children from people who deserve to have them. I have to say my three sons do right by me. Sometimes too right, if you know what I mean, always fussing over me. It's ok, I love them all dearly.

"I need one more promise from you before you go. You must write to me and visit when you can. I know you'll be busy with your tour company and all. You are always welcome."

"Yes, ma'am. I will be glad to." Hank was not given to idle promises.

As he got up to leave Jane said, "Oh, I almost forgot."

She went onto the next room and returned carrying the JLK volume of the latest edition of the *Encyclopedia Britannica.*

"This is for you. It's a loan. Read about your heritage, Hank. Bring it back when you have the time. It's selfish, I know, burdening you with the obligation to come back. But I speak for two people who want to see you again, the one in my head and this old lady standing here before you."

He did not protest as he did with Mr. Gregg who had proffered the book on business, which had set him on a new career path. That tome resulted in fateful change for many a person, most notably for himself. This one would do the same.

"I'll keep it safe, Jane, and bring it back as soon as I can. Thank you. Much obliged for everything. You are a mighty kind woman."

She watched as he rode off, staring after him long after he passed from view.

Jane died three weeks later. Her eldest son, Joe Jr., sent word to Hank in San Antonio. When he came to her funeral, he carried the volume with him.

After the service Joe went over to him. "Hank," he said, "My mother was an extraordinary woman. I'm sure you know that. You don't need to return that book. She wanted you to have the entire set. I'll bring the encyclopedias into town when I come to get supplies next week."

Hank had acquired his heritage. He now had his own story. He read the section on Judaism in the *Britannica* and was startled to learn that the religion was passed down through the mother. That was a shock right there. He still had much to learn and a duty to perform.

A month after the funeral he boarded the train to Houston. Hank found his mother's grave at the cemetery Jane had named. *Anna Miriam Müeller* the headstone read. *Loving wife.* No dates were carved into it. He carried three small rocks with him, which he placed on her stone marker.

Chapter 10:
Nob Hill, San Francisco. May 15, 1904

(Eight Years Earlier or Thereabouts. The Past)

A Tale of Two Lives

You might think that a composition about crime, death, sacrifice and redemption should start with Victor Hugo's *Les Misérables*. Afterall, most essayists would have read the novel and been captured by its relentless devotion to those themes. However, I'd like to try a different tack. I think I am like Mr. Whitman, who told the story of life through poetry, unvarnished in all its human glory and frailty. I hope that Beth approves.

When I received word that my father had died, I was fifteen years old. The headmaster, Mr. Edgar James, pulled me out of class one day and delivered the news. He did it in so a dispassionate fashion you would think he lacked the part of the brain that housed compassion. He drove me out to the farm in his buggy. A few neighbors had gathered on Crabb's

Hill around the hole in the ground where my father's casket would be buried. A Lutheran minister presided over the ceremony. He was an austere man, thin, tall, and dressed in a black suit with a white clerical collar around his neck. It's odd, isn't it, the clarity of images you recall from times like these? I have no idea what he said. I wasn't listening, lost in my own thoughts. I hadn't seen my father for almost a year. He rarely came to see me, except to take me home at Easter and Christmas and, of course, for the summer. I would do all the chores he assigned, always hopeful he would show some sign of affection. He never did. Someone handed me a purse, containing the money my father had stashed away. I took it without a word. The rest was a blur.

I left the school right after that and used part of my meagre inheritance to purchase a horse and saddle. I had no idea where I was going or what I would do when I got there.

A couple of days out of Castle Hills, I ran into three boys on horseback.

"You look a sorry sight," one of them said. "Not worth a-robbin'. What's your name, boy?" They looked only a few years older than me, scruffy and dusty, all of them.

I invented it then and there, "Hank, Hank Miller." Where that came from, I'll never know. One thing I do know is that it fit me just fine, like a well-tailored suit. I wanted a new identity. The old one was too scratchy and worn.

"Why don't you join us then? We're off to Boulder Canyon."

"What's in Boulder Canyon?" I asked.

"Why that's where Emmanuel Clement has his ranch. Don't you know nothing, boy?" Clement, a notable outlaw in his own right, I later learned, was kin to John Wesley Hardin who sometimes would show up at the ranch whenever he found the need to lay low. The whole country knew who Hardin was, a drunken, hardened killer.

Even though it was true that I knew almost nothing, I still took offense. "I know a lot of things. I can read and write and do sums, lots of them."

The three of them laughed at that. "Come on with us. We'll have us a good ole time together."

Having nowhere else to go, I joined up with them. The property was at the end of a blind canyon, filled with its namesake boulders on its floor and lining the slopes above it. The ranch itself was a collection of shacks, a broken-down barn and a corral to keep the horses. Its advantage was the stream that ran down the rocks from an underground spring. They introduced me to Mr. Clement.

"How do, boy. Ready for a life of crime?" He chuckled. "Go get yourself some grub."

Angry at the life I had, hungry and with no prospects, I accepted the invitation. I ate the beans that would be a staple of my diet for the next two years. And I entered into a life of crime.

Six months later I followed Mr. Clement and his gang all the way to a new hideout outside of Laredo. He had got wind that the sheriff in San Antonio had learned of our where-abouts and was forming a posse to come and clean out the Boulder Canyon den of thieves. So, we packed up, not that there was much to pack, and lit out. There was no need for gunplay if it could be avoided. And none of us wanted to get ourselves killed.

It was the Ake brothers who saved me from a life as an outlaw, which otherwise would have likely come to an abbreviated end. After a slow start to success, I became a Wells Fargo guard, riding shotgun for a stagecoach, lawman, and tour operator. It was in that latter role that I met my wife. But that is a story for another day, one that Beth knows all too well and does not bear repeating to her. What haunted me is that I killed seven people along the way. Oh, I almost forgot. I had traveled to places that the boy in me could never even have dreamed about.

These stories I tell are those of a boy and then a man trying to escape his past while simultaneously trying to find it. By that I mean I could never escape the shame I felt as a six-year-old boy running away from a fight. I could not shake the nagging guilt I felt about rustling cattle and killing other human beings. It did not matter that they were bad men or that they were trying to kill me. The rational part of my mind told me that I did what I had to do to survive. The emotional part whispered that's what evil men tell themselves. That's what lower animals do. Was I no more than a devious polecat? Polecat, a word which we Westerners use to describe the liars, the ones likely to shoot us in the back. At the same time I wanted to know my story, my full story. Deep down, I knew that there was more to me than being an outlaw and a cold-blooded killer. The fact that I enforced the law and saved lives was a comfort at times but could not completely assuage the guilt. I had been at war with myself. I hoped that it would not be as destructive to me as the War Between the States had been to the country.

Uriah Heap, that's who I think of when recalling Mr. Clement, collecting a gang of boys to do his dirty work. I escaped the path he had set me on by sheer luck. Mr. Dickens often utilized propitious coincidence in his books, especially in *Great Expectations.* I felt a kinship with Pip. I always regarded myself as lucky. And I had a secret patron of my own. I had somehow survived encounters most men wouldn't have. How to account for it then? While I never felt I deserved it, good fortune seemed to follow me everywhere I went. Perhaps G-d has been watching over me, but not necessarily for my sake. Maybe He chose to protect me, in order that I could protect others. Was I worthy of his shield? That I remain unsure of to this day.

I finally found peace and a path to redemption in the words of an elderly woman who had befriended the mother I never knew. I had signed an armistice with the warring factions in my brain. I sealed that pact in a formal treaty with myself after meeting Beth. Like all men, I will always wonder whether I am truly worthy of the treasures life has bestowed upon me: Beth, the children, loyal friends, and prosperity.

If I am truly worthy, I ask myself, would I be willing to make the sacrifice that Sydney Carton did. I can think of no more an appropriate way to conclude this piece than with his words.

"I see the lives for which I lay down my life, peaceful, useful, prosperous and happy ... I see that I hold a sanctuary in their hearts, and in the hearts of their descendants, generations hence ... I see a child ... who bore my name, a man winning up in the path of life which once was mine. I see the blots I threw upon it, faded away ... I hear him tell the child my story, with a tender and faltering voice.

"It is a far, far better thing that I do, than I have ever done; it is a far, far better rest that I go to, than I have ever known."

I hope and pray that should I have to lay down my life for something, it should be for something noble. I would like to think that at the end I would possess the grace and courage of Mr. Carton.

Chapter 11:
Tangier, Morocco. July 18, 1912

(The Present)

The Rif

E verything takes longer than expected when traveling. Even more when preparing a military campaign. So it was that the expedition did not start out until four days after *The Beth* had docked, instead of the two they had planned for. The Middle East worked on a different time frame than San Francisco and certainly on a different one than New York.

Eager to be on their way, the armed caravan set out on its intended journey two hours after dawn, nearly two hours after Hank and Figgins had counted on. It was not an auspicious start to a mission that relied on timing. A recalcitrant mule had objected to its load and had to be cajoled into line by its handler. One of the horses stepped on the foot of an inattentive porter who required bandaging. The guides were late yet pleased with themselves for arriving early by their standards.

Unlike the Americans, Figgins was accustomed to the inevitable delays common to this part of the world. He knew they were bound to occur at the most inauspicious times and counseled patience to his three comrades-in-arms. For their part the Millers hoped that this ill-timed tardiness would not derail the mission. Hank was relieved to finally get started. In an earlier time he might have said that he was itchin' to get a goin'. Now, though, he kept his sense of relief to himself.

The father and son piloting them led, riding side by side. Next came Hank and Figgins, followed by the twins. The animal drivers handled the mules. A cook and two porters, all cousins, brought up the rear on their animals. They would face both easy and hard terrain ahead and believed they had properly prepared. Hank had faith that the colonel and his trusted guides knew what they were doing, despite the anxiety of the slow start. After all, he reminded himself, he had experienced delays before. A broken wheel, a horse that went lame, a misplaced train car. None of that had ever happened at a good time. However, he couldn't escape the notion that none of those mishaps had ever posed a threat to his life.

They camped that night outside of Tangier. The guides and the four foreigners took turns guarding the encampment. They couldn't be too careful. Even though Jasmina's husband had sent messengers out in advance to bribe the tribes of the Rif to assure safe passage, you never knew what might lay ahead.

What lay ahead was Raisuli.

"Pops, those riders on both ridges have been tracking us for hours now." It was Ben who spoke. "What do you think their intentions are?"

"I sure don't know, son. I've been watching, same as you. Figgins, what do you think?" It was the one person Hank now routinely addressed by his last name.

"My best guess is that they are scouts for a much larger party. They want to follow us to better assess whether the things we are transporting are worth the effort it might take to secure them. I think our arms are sufficiently visible to at least ward off an immediate attack. They have a calculation to perform, a risk reward ratio. They might take into account the potential customer who will receive the goods. These brigands may not want to risk the ire of that customer."

"Well, that last part at least is reassuring," Hank replied.

Minutes later a figure on a polished black Arabian appeared on the crest to their right.

"Forget what I said. That's Sharif Mulai Ahmed er Raiuni, better known as Raisuli. Nasty brigand. He is the leader of the Jabala tribe. He favors kidnapping to raise funds over raiding caravans. You may recall the Perdicaris affair in 1904. Terrible business, terrible. Your Teddy Roosevelt made hay with it. 'Perdicaris alive or Raisuli dead,' was a favorite campaign slogan of his. Sent the fleet, he did, to Tangier. Wonder, I still do, how a battleship would find its way to the middle of the Rif. It was rumored that he sent along the Winchester that Raisuli demanded as a part of the enormous ransom that was paid. The good news is that Raisuli is a man of his word. He returns his captives, at least the foreign ones, upon receipt of payment." Before any of the others could interrupt to ask the obvious question, he continued, "The bad news is that he'll likely burn your eyes out, if not paid."

Hank spoke in his most laconic Texan, "Well, sir. I aim to keep my sight." He undid the flap of the holster that held his new Colt.

"I don't advise gunplay if we can avoid it. There are too many of them. Raisuli does not like Europeans. Our freedom or survival might depend on his attitude toward you Americans. He is likely to send an emissary to better assess the situation. He'll then decide whether to attack or merely try to frighten us into surrender. We are worth a fortune to him."

"Pops, we aren't going to surrender," was the definitive answer from both twins, spoken as they often did in unison.

"Of course not, boys. Whatever gave you an idea like that? I'd rather get myself bit by a rattlesnake than submit to those devils. Let's wait and see what those varmints have up their sleeve."

Hank had reverted to a manner of speech he had worked hard over the years to divest himself from. He had long ago settled into a comfortable western lilt of a type that inspires confidence in others. It was one that projected confidence.

Figgins for his part did not know what to make of Hank's apparently newfound speech pattern. He looked at him with bewilderment. The twins, likewise, were baffled. They could not tell whether their father was trying to inject humor to help diffuse a tense situation or had simply lapsed into familiar cadences in the face of danger.

Hank smiled at all of them, gathered together as they were on horseback. "Don't worry, gentlemen. I haven't forgotten the English language. I was rehearsing." He glanced at Figgins and continued. "I have all my faculties. We will figure a way out of this mess, whether by word or bullet." He was not as confident as he sounded. But hearing that from their father reassured the boys.

About a half hour later, a figure on horseback rode down the embankment on their right. It was a skillful descent. The man, however, was not an emissary as Figgins had predicted. Raisuli himself cantered toward them, not more than one hundred yards away. He was an imposing sight riding a regal black Arabian stallion. It was a fitting mount for a man who could trace his bloodline to the Prophet Mohammed. He was burly with a hint of gray in his substantial beard. A red and white keffiyeh topped his head. He carried a Winchester Model 1873, on his back, slung crosswise. It was the scimitar in its scabbard, however, that drew their attention.

As he approached, Hank resisted the impulse to withdraw his Henry from its own scabbard. The four foreigners lined up alongside one another. The two guides, brave men both, chose to sit their horses a few paces behind the quartet. Raisuli could inspire fear in anyone familiar with his reputation. They had chosen an intermediate position, not in front but not cowering at the back of the line.

The sharif halted his steed not ten feet from the riders. A grand smile crossed his face. "Welcome, gentlemen. What took you so long?"

"Colonel Figgins, I see you have decided to reacquaint yourself with my country? Have you found it much changed?"

"No sir, I have not. It remains as enchanting as ever."

"Ah, as charming as ever. Well, at least you are not the French or the bloody Germans. And you three must be the Millers." Turning his head slightly he said, "The famous cowboy, Hank, no? These two must be your boys. I'm afraid I don't know their names."

Hank introduced them. "This is David and this is Ben." The two tipped their hats and nodded in turn.

"You must have trouble telling them apart." He turned to the boys, "Plenty of opportunity for mischief, no? Who could tell you apart? Well, maybe one of your western girls could tell the difference in your kisses, hmm. Tried that trick did you, kiss the same one on different occasions?"

The twins could not help the broad grins that appeared on their faces. They blushed and laughed aloud.

Then, it was Figgins turn, "I should have known you would have spies everywhere. I see no point in inquiring about the source of your information."

"I will tell you anyway. I pay the customs officials and dock workers to inform me of the comings and goings at the port. And the manager at the Hotel Continental is a cousin of mine. If you tell anyone, I will have your tongues cut out." His face grew menacing.

Their smiles, product of the previous teasing, quickly transformed to frowns. How quickly upward turned lips could wheel downward.

"Come gentleman. I jest. I do not cut out tongues." He paused for dramatic effect, "I burn out eyes." Then he continued, "I have no intention of harming any of you. I am Lord of the Rif. You are my guests. You will not be held hostage. Figgins served here with honor and did what he could to oppose the French and Germans. He was a good soldier. And you, Mr. Miller. Words of your exploits have reached even this distant country. I wonder did you really kill over a dozen men?"

"Seven … so far." It was Raisuli's turn to be puzzled by a remark laden with truth and delivered with an ambiguity of intent.

He went on after a brief hesitation, "I see. No harm will come to any of you. You have my word. Please, you will join me for dinner and go on your way in the morning. Free as birds as you say in America. I look forward to hearing about your adventures in your wild West over a most humble meal."

It was in fact a feast, of many courses, one with spiced lamb as the star attraction.

As the last course of dates, apples with honey, and figs was presented, Raisuli leaned over to Hank and Figgins. Both occupied places of honor and were the first to be served every course. "My spies were unable to determine what exactly you carry in those crates. Or your destination. I fear it is the fortress in Zinat, belonging to that pig Ahmed. Calls himself Pasha. Ha. He is no pasha. I knew his father well. An honorable man. That was how I learned of Mr. Miller's previous adventure here. From him. You are a brave soul, Mr. Miller."

Figgins was the first to answer. "Sir, I am afraid I cannot tell you what we carry. What I can say is that our mission is an honorable one. It will do no harm to you or your people. You might even benefit from it one day. Please keep that in mind."

"I will indeed, Figgins. And you, Mr. Miller, do you plan to rescue another of your damsels in distress? A gunfight perhaps?"

"No gunplay if I can avoid it. I've had more than enough of that. I carry a Colt and a Henry in hopes of preventing a fight. They can be great intimidators. It's what the doctor ordered to scare away fleas with guns, wanting to make a name for themselves." He did not mention that there was, in fact, a young girl in need of rescue. And he wanted at all costs to avoid a gunfight.

"And you two young men. Will you follow in your father's footsteps?"

"We could never follow in his footsteps, sir," said Ben. "He has cast too large a footprint to try to fit into. He is too great a man. We would sink so deep in his tracks that we might never get out. No, we will take a path of our own, the law perhaps."

Then it was David's turn. He looked at his father as he spoke.

"I am also thinking of the law. And as my brother said, my father is a great man."

Hank had never heard those sentiments from them before. Ever. They had always engaged in good natured ribbing as adults, but not full-on praise of this magnitude. He was embarrassed. He would never admit he was glowing with inner pride that his boys would think of him in this way.

Later that night the brothers went off by themselves. They had matters to discuss. David, exercising his prerogative as the senior of the two, started. "We have to protect pops at all costs. He is the key to us succeeding. And mother would be devastated if he didn't make it back."

"I don't know about you, but I'm willing to take a bullet on his behalf," Ben replied.

"Let's hope it never comes to that."

They walked back to the encampment arm in arm.

At virtually the same time Hank took Figgins aside. He recalled what he had written about Sydney Carton. That had been fiction. This was not. "If it comes to it and you have a choice to save me or my sons, you know what you must do. I've lived a goodly portion of my life. They haven't. Besides, their mother would be heartbroken should they not return alive. Promise me Figgins."

"I promise my friend."

As the expedition was about to depart the next morning Sharif Mulai Ahmed er Raiuni came to see them off. "My men will assure your safe passage to Zinat and back. I thank you, my friends, for sharing a meal with me. May Allah protect you. Oh, I almost forgot. I advise you not to return to the Rif or to Morocco for that matter. I do not know what the state of my finances would be. I have a whole tribe under my care. I, perhaps, would see it as my responsibility to hold you for ransom. Mr. Miller, you are a mine of gold as you Americans say. The Colonel, maybe not so much.

Your reputation precedes you. What American president would fail to pay a handsome sum to save your life?"

"Well, sir, as much as I admire your country, we will all heed your advice. But I don't think you're right about my worth. I don't reckon the U.S. Treasury values me a plumb nickel."

"Go with Allah," was the last Raisuli said as he waved a farewell. Hank, Figgins, and the boys nodded in return.

Chapter 12:
San Antonio, Texas. April 10, 1890

(Twenty-two Years Earlier or Thereabouts. The Past)

The World Changes

Part One—Fateful Encounters

H istorians mark 1890 as the end of the western frontier. What they really mean is that the white man had so devastated the Native American population that they no longer posed a threat. This is not to say that the original inhabitants of the continent were blameless. No, not at all. There were cruelties enough by both sides in what came to be known collectively as the Indian Wars. Nonetheless, for good or evil, it was the white man who prevailed. It was he, though, that had trouble keeping the promises he made. Greed all too often overcame integrity.

There were other things to indicate that the collective manifest destiny of the nation had indeed arrived: a cross country railroad and with it a uniform nationwide timekeeping system, the telegraph, and the integration of the territories from Mexico. The notion that we were no longer a collection of states but rather a United States, had for the most part taken root after the Civil War. A few exceptions hung on to antiquated concepts of the country as an assemblage of sovereignties bound by a bare minimum of constitutional obligations. Texas, of course, was one of them. To be fair, that huge state went along as best its independent spirit could manage.

End of the frontier and a coast to coast unified nation or no, the legacy of slavery would haunt the nation for decades after the war that ended it. As a child Hank had been taught it was the natural order of things. The teachers at the James School for Boys back in Castle Hills said that the White man was superior to the Black and therefore had the God given right to enslave him. The bible itself endorsed the practice, it did. Or so they said.

As a child Hank had no way of knowing better. He had no one at home to tell him anything different than the standard orthodoxy used in homes, schools, and churches to justify the practice. His father was not a slave owner. He rarely spoke about anything, much less about the "peculiar institution." And a conversation of that sort or any sort was unimaginable. Hank had no occasion to think about it until he met Jim Handy.

Handy was the town blacksmith and farrier in Laredo during Hank's first year as sheriff there. Hank would board his Appaloosa, Charlie, in the stable adjacent to the smithy.

Handy owned both. He was a tall man, his arms heavily muscled as you would expect of a smith.

"Howdy there, Sheriff. What can I do you for?"

"Well Jim. Charlie here has thrown a shoe."

"Come on over to the barn with me. We'll see about taking care of it."

Except for passing a pleasantry or two, they had never said much to each other, leastways until now.

They entered the stable and Handy pointed to a stall on the left, "Park him in there, and I'll take a look." He carried his kit with him: clinch to remove the shoe, pincers to remove the nails, rasp to even the hoof, hammer, nails and replacement shoes. He made his own horseshoes to meticulous standards. He would decide whether the shoes he had on hand would fit. Likely not, he knew. Handy would almost certainly have to fashion a custom made one at his forge.

Jim Handy was a friendly but not very talkative man. No one in town knew much about him other than the fact he was more than competent at his profession. He lived in a small home, a mile outside of town with his wife and four children. Julia homeschooled them. She took in laundry to earn extra cash. The daughter of enslaved parents, she was the fourth of five surviving children. Her parents toiled together in Galveston before the war and were among the first to be set free when General Granger issued his fateful order. They had worked their way west, enrolling themselves and their children in the newly created Freedman Schools along the way. Julia wanted to be a teacher herself one day.

Handy hesitated before getting started with his work. He stared at Hank before asking, "Sheriff, you carry a reputation for honesty and fairness. Do you mind if I ask you a question about the law?"

"Sure Jim. What exactly do you have in mind?" Hank had copies of the 1879 edition of *Revised Statutes* and the latest of *The Penal Code and Code of Criminal Procedure* in his office. If he didn't have an answer on hand, he could always look it up.

What possessed him to go on like that Handy never quite knew. He rarely if ever spoke to white folk the way he opened up that day to Hank. A sense about the man, he later reflected, had told him that it was safe.

"Sheriff, I did work for a farmer I won't name a few weeks back. Made him three barrels, a plow, a hoe, and a shovel. I wondered why he would want me to make the tools because he could have gone to Mr. Hatigrove's store to buy them, all except the plow which would need to be ordered. I didn't want to be impolite and ask. And I can always use extra money. We set a price. He never took my hand to shake on it. When he returned to pick up his goods, I loaded up his wagon. He set off without paying me. I called after him. But he wouldn't stop. I rode out there two days ago to try and collect my money. I wasn't twenty yards from his front door when he came out armed with a scattergun aimed right at me. Called me a word I won't say aloud and told me to get off his property. I had no interest in facing down that shotgun, but I did tell him that I expected payment as agreed upon and left. What is it I can do? It's not just the money. That man owes me my pride. I've finally about run out of patience with people who treat me less than a man. Things have to change. They have to."

"Jim, I'm not sure which statute exactly this falls under, and whether it's a civil matter or a criminal one or both. Seems to me it's a stew with lots of vittles mixed together. I'll have me a ride out there tomorrow and see if I can get this sorted. Why didn't you come to me sooner?"

That last question seemed to anger Handy. "Sheriff, in case you didn't notice, I'm a Black man. Your laws don't apply in the same way to folks like me and mine."

Hank was taken aback. He had come across many Black cowboys in his travels. He had worked with several on Mr. Pickett's ranch. They were hard working and as good as any at breaking horses or punching cows. He knew the accounts of the famed Buffalo soldiers. It was that he really hadn't given much thought to the unequal treatment parceled out to them. It was the way of things. He hadn't thought twice about calling the man standing before him Jim, instead of Mr. Handy, as he did white men older than himself. A dozen thoughts like that shot through his head. A sudden anger gripped him. It was not directed at Handy. It was squarely aimed at that dumb ole Hank Miller.

As if talking to himself, "Well sir, not in my town, no sir. Jim, er, Mr. Handy. Come by in the early morning. We're gonna ride out to that farmer of yours together and get this here issue settled."

It might not have been the best decision he ever made, but it was the right one. He knew by experience never to trust one man's side to any story. Like as not, the tales men would tell in a dispute over money or women had more sides to 'em than a fancy carousel, all atwistin' and aturnin'. It would be better to go out there alone and get Ames' version of events.

That was the smart move. It was one a savvy lawman would take. But in this case what Jim Handy said rang true. He knew the farmer would not like the fact that he brought the smith with him. The more Hank thought about it, the better he liked that idea, shotgun, or no.

"I'll have your horse ready, even if I have to work all night," the tall blacksmith said with a broad smile on his face.

Hank knew he had some hard pondering to do and had a difficult time sleeping that night. He was disturbed, disturbed at himself for his ignorance. "How in tarnation could I have lived so long in a fog like this? It's as if the morning sun never rose to shine and burn off that heavy mist that clouded my vision. Well, I'm a-gonna let that light surround me now."

They reached the Ames' farm mid-morning the next day. The farmer had seen them coming and left the mule pulled plow in the field to meet the two riders.

"Howdy sheriff. What brings you out to these parts? Why do you have that boy in tow?"

For a second Hank contemplated voicing an angry response but held his tongue. Jim, for his part, remained stoic, his expression neutral. Both men stayed on their mounts. They seemed to take a degree of pleasure in looking down on their quarry.

"Mr. Ames, Mr. Handy here tells me you owe him for the tools he made for you. Is that right?" When Ames did not answer, he continued on, his bile rising. "I tell you now. Who I choose to ride with is none of your concern. And Mr. Handy here is no boy. He is a full-grown man with a family and a business of his own."

Chastised, Ames continued in a less confrontational tone. "I didn't pay, it's true, Sheriff. I had call not to. Those tools of his were shoddy work. I don't pay for shoddy work."

Hank now knew the truth of the matter. Handy did not make shoddy anything. His work was meticulous. He saw that for himself many a time.

"Well, let's go take a look at that shoddy work, Mr. Ames."

They dismounted and did just that. "Mr. Ames, we both know the quality of these tools and that plow. You are in violation of Texas penal code C104.7. You have also come afoul of enough civil codes to spend a month in court, defending yourself or hiring a lawyer to do that for you. I could haul you off to jail right now if I choose." Hank wanted to be sure of the facts before applying what he had learned. He had studied Texas law the night before and had come armed with that knowledge.

That was enough to encourage the farmer to agree to pay in exchange for avoiding court or jail time. Spending days in the calaboose was not an appealing alternative, and paying a lawyer was certainly beyond his means. He gave Handy a down payment of twenty dollars and promised to deliver the rest the following week.

They rode off without another word. Hank would spend many pleasant evenings at the Handy dinner table, enjoying Julia's fine cooking. Years later, when it came time to start his tour company, he knew exactly the person he wanted to join his merry band.

***

Jim Handy had moved his family to San Antonio a year before Hank arrived. They sold their home and business in Laredo. Julia had wanted to be closer to her family for a long time. And she wanted to teach. He reopened a forge and a stable on the city's East Side where many former slaves had established Freedmen's Towns. There was still a need for the services he provided as blacksmith in the San Antonio of 1887. Julia accepted a teaching position at a Freedman's School she had always known she was meant for. When Hank came calling, they enjoyed a happy reunion and embarked upon a business arrangement.

It had turned out quite differently than Hank expected. He had begun to run short of cash. Near about everything cost more than expected. If he ever had a chance of getting the business off the ground, he would need additional funding. The local bank had already turned him down. Who on earth was Hank? He was new to town. Who would vouch for him? So, Hank offered to make Jim a partner in his venture. All it would take was a small investment. For Hank this was not solely a business decision. He trusted Jim and valued him as a friend. Who better to work with? For Jim it represented far more than another source of income. It was a way to pay back the investment Hank had made in him. He didn't like owing a debt. And most importantly, they were friends. Friends helped out one another. They shook hands on the deal. Jim would take a ten percent interest in exchange for the money he would invest. And he would join *The American West Tour Company's* cast of characters as a part time player. He liked the role Hank had outlined for him. It would be fun. And he enjoyed modifying the wagon that would carry their guests on tours, for a fair price of course. That was important to both of them.

***

It was the tenth of April, 1890, a little over a year since Jane had died. That encounter had changed his life, allowing him to begin a reconciliation with the warring parties inside his head. Hank now stood at the San Antonio train station, waiting for his latest clients, guests to his mind, to arrive. His tours had earned a reputation as providing an exciting and authentic western experience. It had even been profitable.

When the Franklins stepped off their private car Hank knew who they must be. Mr. Franklin was the first to touch down. He was of medium height, dressed in a herringbone gray suit with bowler style hat atop his graying hair that peaked out at the sides and black shoes that were so highly polished that they could be mistaken for giant ebony cultured pearls. The woman he helped down must be his wife. He offered a hand to her as she descended the three steps from the train. Dressed in a stylish and tailored lavender lady's suit, bustled in the back, she was a youngish matron with a pale complexion. Last came Elizabeth the daughter. She was stunning: the brightest blue eyes Hank had ever seen, raven black hair down to her shoulders, bright blue silk dress as if molded to her figure. Hank couldn't help himself. He could not help but stare. He felt himself focus on her in the same way he had done with those murderers from his days at Wells Fargo or with Sam Bass, the vengeful gunslinger he had killed in Laredo. For a brief moment he saw nothing else except her.

He was bewildered by the effect she had on him. Surely that slip of a girl posed no danger. Nevertheless, he again found himself clutching that locket in his left pants pocket. Little did he know what peril he was actually in. Their eyes met, and she was not the first to avert them. He quickly recovered himself, embarrassed by his own brashness. Staring at the daughter of his well-heeled clients was not a smart business practice. Her parents did not fail to notice.

Elizabeth had persuaded them to answer the ad Hank had placed in *The Philadelphia Inquirer*. She finally cajoled the staid pair into submission. It was, after all, to be a celebration of her twenty-first birthday and graduation from college. As a child Elizabeth had held romantic notions of the western frontier, ever since reading about the exploits of the heroes who populated the pages of the periodicals and dime novels of her childhood. Ned Buntline had been her favorite as a schoolgirl. Her father was a successful attorney, the son of two school teachers, and a distant cousin of Benjamin, the most famous of all Philadelphia's residents ever to be. Her mother, Elizabeth Agnes Astor Adams, brought a considerable dowry and later an inheritance to their marriage. She was a distant relative of two presidents and a closer one to John Jacob Astor, accounting for both the blue color of her blood and the wealth it contained.

Recovering himself and putting on his best Texas smile, Hank walked over to them. He had dressed in costume, a cowboy like figure of the West he thought folks from back East had come to expect. In reality what he wore that day wasn't that very different from his everyday garb. He was the real thing, no matter that he believed he was playing a part.

That part was him, down to his core. He introduced himself, tipping his newly bought Stetson to the ladies and shaking hands with the father. Hank half expected that man to have a look at his teeth, the way a cowpoke would do of a horse he was fixing to buy. He didn't cotton to being inspected up and down the way Mr. Franklin was doing. It rankled. He held his tongue as he usually did in these types of provocative circumstances and greeted his guests, "Welcome to San Antonio. I truly hope you enjoy your stay with us." He doffed his broad brimmed hat and gave a slight bow. He had reserved a suite for them at the magnificent Menger Hotel, built adjacent to the Alamo, shrine to Texas independence. Sam Houston, hero of that war with Mexico, had stayed there. So had Lee and Grant, making it appealing to those who had fought on both sides of the great conflict.

"I expect you are all tired from your long journey. I have a buggy outside to take you to your hotel."

Franklin nodded to Hank's entreaty. The three of them followed him to the carriage.

It had been a long journey. Franklin had reluctantly taken a two-month hiatus from his law practice to please his only child. He left it in the hands of his partners. They had stopped in Chicago, St. Louis, and Dallas, taking the circuitous train routes that would eventually land them in San Antonio. Traveling by private car whenever possible and the rest in their own compartments, it was not as grueling a journey as other, less affluent individuals would have faced. They stayed in elegant lodgings after each leg of the trip. It helped them quickly recover, if indeed recover was the proper term for the travails of travel endured in opulent, private railway cars. And

Elizabeth was bursting with boundless energy. That was the actual exhausting part for her parents. They had taken her to Great Britain and the European mainland. But none of them had been this far west before. It was truly an adventure for her, if not for them. They agreed to it for her sake, not theirs. They had no interest in consorting with the primitive frontiersmen of the American West.

That night, safely ensconced in their hotel room, and once the two of them were alone, Mrs. Franklin admonished her daughter, "Elizabeth, I want you to stay away from that man. I saw the way he looked at you. For all we know he could be dangerous. If nothing else, he is an as yet unclassified species of ruffian. Uncouth at the very least. You will stay close to your father at all times. I was reluctant to come here in the first place. I argued with him. But I knew in the end he would indulge you."

"Oh mother," hoping to assuage her mother's fears, "I don't know the look you are talking about. Besides, Cousin John already sent us the letter vouching for the safety of the tour."

Her father might have been indulgent, but he wasn't anything, if not thorough and cautious. He had the tour company and its owner investigated. Fortunately, his sources didn't go back quite enough into Hank's past, or he would never have agreed. All he knew was that the business was reputable. Several cousins living in New York had taken the trip and had confirmed that it lived up to the brochure. They had felt themselves safe at all times.

"Don't worry. I will remain detached, both in tenor and distance." She wasn't sure that this was the approach she

would actually take. That scar on the side of his head
certainly was intriguing, but it was not the only thing that
interested her. It would be almost three years before she
learned how that scar got there in the first place.

Hank had arranged for them to set out two days later, not
the very next day. He never wanted to rush his guests before
they became accustomed to their surroundings. The road he
chose would take them through the hamlet of Castle Hills
into its namesake Hill Country. The area had been peaceful
for years, the Native Americans no longer a threat to settlers.
The occasional outlaw still roamed the outskirts of civilization but never along the routes that Hank had chosen. He
picked them for their natural beauty and their historical significance. Hank liked to surprise his guests with the lovely
scenery that surrounded San Antonio. They had expected
grassy plains or dry desert dotted with cactus and populated
by rattlesnakes. There was certainly that, of course. But the
landscapes held a whole lot more, from richly green hills to
the flowing creeks. Those features would delight the tourists,
expressing surprise at the interesting and diverse scenery the
area held. He liked to point out the wildlife at San Pedro
Creek which always fascinated his visitors: red-shoulder
hawk, yellow-crowned night-heron; yes, night-heron in central Texas. There were roadrunners, armadillos, an occasional
coyote, and a rare bobcat. And then there was the live oak,
Ashe juniper, pecan trees with the roadway lined by
Bluebonnet and Indian Paintbrush in all their glory. It was as
if nature itself had placed them there to entertain weary travelers. The hunters had finished off the bison, and the farmers
had cleared vast numbers of native trees and bushes; but

much remained. Hank had become something of a naturalist, first by design to entertain, and shortly afterward by keen interest.

He would always start his tour at the Alamo, spinning tales of Davy Crockett and General Santa Anna. He had put that encyclopedia of Jane's to good use. But it was Julia who wrote the script he would recite. She wrote it in a way that would best suit Hank's persona and crafted a version of events that she knew not to be entirely true. Stick to the legend that had grown around it. She thus left out a few notable historical facts. It was a tale, however, she thought would please the tourists. She knew that to many Texans that battle occurred yesterday, not fifty years ago. They were proud of their eventual victory in the war that would result in their independence. It would do no good for business to offend any one of them. You never knew when a Texan might show up.

Hank enjoyed the little touches Julia added that the *Britannica* did not. That Mexican general was an odd one all right, once holding a burial ceremony for the leg he lost in battle. Hank at first chose to omit these sorts of gory details, so as not to offend the delicate sensibilities of his guests. From their questions, however, he learned that they actually reveled in them, always wanting more. Of course, that was one secret to his success, always leave them wanting more. He took to inventing or embellishing those bloody details when the historical record or local lore were silent on the matter. He sprinkled his tales with little known facts or, truth be told, doubtful but colorful asides about the desperados who roamed the frontier. His campsite yarns were a tourist favorite. He never talked about his role in any of it.

Somehow, that didn't sit right with him. Inevitably, an enthusiastic youngster would ask if he had ever shot anybody. He would answer truthfully and let the matter drop. Little did he anticipate that a couple of those very same desperados would return to haunt the territory and one day find him.

***

Every few years, after financial success had come to him, Hank would gather up his brood and return to San Antonio. He would lead them on an expedition into the backcountry. He enjoyed the quiet the desert night would bring, disturbed on occasion by the howl of the lone coyote calling to its mate. Beth would point out the constellations in the sky, their brilliance undiminished by the artificial lights of civilization. Hank would name the vegetation they passed. He identified the birds that flew by or nested above in the trees. He called out the names of the fish they saw in the streams and brooks of the Hill Country. But those were times yet to come. He and Beth would first need to survive their encounter with death incarnate.

***

Hank was there to meet his guests as he always did at the entrance to their hotel. "Good morning to you all. I trust you slept well last night."

Elizabeth was the lone Franklin to reply. "We did. Thank you, Mr. Miller." Her parents nodded, their faces set as if a chisel would have a hard time carving a smile onto them.

"Let me introduce Edgy, our cook. You will be amazed by what he can whip up out on the trail."

In response, the three of them took on dubious expressions.

"Step up on up here," he said, pointing to the stool that would help them onto the cushioned seats lining either side of the open wagon.

Edgy sat at the front, doubling as cook and driver. Tied to the back of it were two horses the guests could ride, if the notion tickled their fancy. Hank rode alongside on Charlie, his faithful Appaloosa.

Hank had Jim outfit the wagon with a clever device that would roll across the metal skeleton above in case of rain or uncomfortable heat from a blazing sun. He named it *The Convertible* and had the name stenciled on the side of the wagon. Jim, in turn, had come up with the idea of special shock absorbers that would make the ride more comfortable. He designed and fashioned them himself.

The five of them started out their excursion at the Alamo, across from the hotel where they were staying. It was a three-acre complex, surrounded by a thick adobe wall. Its centerpiece was the chapel, a sand-colored structure of typical Spanish design with ornate sculptures on either side of its heavy wooden doors. It was only moments after Hank began his narrative that Mr. Franklin interrupted him, "We are familiar with the history of the place, *Hank*. There is no need to go on."

Elizabeth pleaded with him, "Please father let him continue his story. I'm sure he has a lot to tell us that we don't know about. He lives here after all. *Please*." She knew just the tone to use to get her way.

As always, Mr. Franklin could not resist the pleadings of his daughter. Elizabeth had graduated at the top of her class at Swarthmore. Her areas of concentration had been English literature and history. However, she had a keen intellect and an unrelenting curiosity, which often led her down arcane byways. She always questioned convention. She was thus a perfect match for a school that chose its own path to higher education, among the first to adopt coeducation. Elizabeth was a self-confident woman, but not given to conceit, which is not to say she didn't allow herself a peek in the mirror. Well, maybe more than a peek. She was well aware of her effect on men. She had fended off any number of suitors, allowing them a brief kiss or three during their fleeting courtships. Beth used that mirror on the wall above the dressing table in her bedroom, but not solely for grooming. It was her instrument of self-reflection. This woman had great expectations for herself, more than she would disclose to her parents or even to her best friends. She was bound for great things but didn't yet know what they were. Beth, as she would come to be called by her future husband, glimpsed something special in Hank that her parents obviously did not. She was not yet sure what it was. But she knew that special could be good or evil.

"All right," Franklin said as he turned back to Hank, and in his most formal tone, "Please continue with your story."

Hank started back as if he had never noticed the rude and abrupt interruption. He donned his folksiest guise and resumed in his best Western drawl, following the script that Julia had written.

"The Alamo was first a mission built in 1724 by the Catholics to convert the Indians," he said as he pointed to the stone chapel. "I guess they were none too successful because they gave up the ghost in 1793." He waited for the expected chuckle that customarily followed his last remark. It did not come. He went on anyway, reciting Julia's version of the saga. "It's best to begin the story of the Alamo by understanding why it was that Texians, that's what they called themselves, Texians, would go to war to be free of Mexico. The Texas War for Independence as it is now called began sometime in October of 1835. American settlers and even many Mexican residents rebelled against a government that they claimed was as unfair to them as the British had been toward their cousins in the colonies. They were plumb fed up with the enforcement of the new Mexican constitution and decided it was time to fight for their freedom. We Texans surely have inherited that independent streak."

Hank paused again for recognition. This time he waited for a nod from anyone in his small audience in order to continue. It was that Texas stubbornness that had finally come out. He continued when each of the Franklins finally gestured.

"Okay, now. Where was I? Oh yeah. Well, next thing you know the Texian army took the mission from a garrison of Mexican soldiers in December of 1835 and left a small number behind. When word reached them that an army under Santa Anna was marching to retake the Alamo, they put out a call for help. They knew that they were not enough to defend the compound. Well, General Sam Houston sent none other than Colonel Jim Bowie with reinforcements. You know old Jim, inventor of the knife that bears his name. I have one right here."

He took the distinct, long bladed knife out of its scabbard to show them. "Fine grade tempered steel. It's made for fighting. And Bowie did use it that way." He did not understand that the elder Franklins were not his typical audience. Or if he did, he kept to the script anyway. What motivated him to do that, he never knew. They reacted with revulsion. That weapon served to reinforce their view that the West was inhabited by utter barbarians, led by the barbarian-in-chief, this man who called himself Hank.

Heedless of the reaction he elicited, Hank sheathed the knife and continued, "Bowie would share command with Colonel William Travis. And Davy Crockett himself answered the call, bringing with him a contingent of volunteers.

"Meanwhile President of Mexico, General Antonio Lopez de Santa Anna, was out for vengeance. He assembled himself an army over seven times the number of defenders and armed with cannon. His forces attacked on February twenty three of 1836. The brave souls inside the makeshift fortress held out until the fifth of March when they were finally overrun. They had inflicted a Texas-sized portion of casualties on the Mexicans, but the overwhelming numbers and the cannon proved too much for that tiny band of heroes. It is said that Davy Crockett's body was found surrounded by no less than sixteen dead Mexican soldiers. Imagine that. Sixteen. The five surviving Americans, out of ammunition, finally surrendered. Santa Anna had them shot by firing squad.

"Any questions about the battle?"

The elder Franklins shook their collective heads, eager to get this well-worn tale done with. Elizabeth, though, looked annoyed.

"But the story does not end there. This was the War for Texas Independence and independence is what they got. Sam Houston got his revenge on April twenty-first at the Battle of San Jacinto. He even took Santa Anna prisoner, mercifully choosing not to execute him in retribution for his murdering of the prisoners he had taken. Instead, in exchange for his freedom El Presidente signed a formal treaty, recognizing Texas as a country of its own. I don't think we ever quite gave up that notion. But the rest, as they say, is history. We ended our brief stint as a nation of our own and joined the Union in 1845."

Hank stopped there, waiting for applause or at least some kind of recognition. It never came.

"Mr. Miller," Elizabeth intoned, "You left out a few pertinent facts."

Hank, stunned, waited for what he knew would be a rebuke. He tried his best not to stare at the woman who was about to deliver a history lesson. He resisted putting his hand in his left pocket to find that locket.

"First of all, Jim Bowie was a slaver and a scoundrel. He left Louisiana to escape his creditors. Second, most of the Americans who rebelled against Mexico had been living in Texas illegally. Even if having been enticed there by the Mexican government. Third, one of their prime motivations in seeking independence was the preservation of slavery. Mexico had outlawed it in 1824. Many of them feared that the authorities would enforce the law, and they would lose their human possessions. Fourth, Santa Anna warned the defenders he would take no prisoners if they did not surrender. Fifth, oh that's enough. I know that the Alamo's defenders were brave men who died for a cause they believed in. There were good men there. Davy Crocket had strenuously opposed Andrew Jackson's decree that led eventually to the Trail of Tears. But that cause they died for was tainted, at least in part. You should tell the whole story, Mr. Miller, not a sanitized version."

Hank knew she was right. But not for his business. He and Julia knew those things and more. He could only respond, "Miss Franklin, you have the truth of it."

He was careful not to make a promise he knew would not, could not, keep. He never said he would alter his chronicle of events.

Early that afternoon they made camp at a spot Hank had specifically chosen for his tour. The site backed into a semi-circular, rocky outcropping that provided shelter and a cozy spot for a cooking fire. He and Edgy tied up the horses. Hank always gave his guests the option of sleeping in the wagon as space permitted or in tents on the ground in the bedrolls he provided. This soil was reasonably soft, consisting mostly of sand, which would provide a comfortable mattress.

They were unloading those bedrolls when Edgy quietly spoke up, "I suppose you seen those riders." Both had earlier spotted the small dust cloud that signified the approach of men on horseback. As the party neared, they could spot at least two. It was the wrong direction for Jim and Tom to be coming from for their theatrical appearance.

Hank went to his three guests now sitting in the collapsible chairs around the campfire. "Folks," he said. "You see those two riders, coming from the north? I'm not sure who they are. I don't want to cause undue alarm, but I'm sending Edgy up there in those rocks with my rifle in case there's trouble." They all stood up and came toward him.

"Hank, Mr. Miller, or whatever you want to be called, if this is a part of the show you told us about, I want no part of it. You are scaring my wife and daughter." In reality, behind the bluster, it was Mr. Franklin who was rattled.

"Mr. Franklin, I assure you this is not a part of the tour. But there is little chance of any real danger. We are just taking precautions. Please go back to your seats over by the wagon." He decided not to add, "where you will be out of the line of fire."

When he stood his ground defiantly refusing to move, Hank raised his voice, "*Go. Now*, Mr. Franklin." He then in fact did say. "Take your wife and daughter and get yourselves out of any line of fire." He lowered his voice a notch. "Please sir, do as I tell you. I know what I'm doing. It is for your own safety and that of your family."

Franklin stood unmoving for just enough time to reclaim his dignity and then led his family to their seats by the fire. No one had ever spoken to him that way, not even the judges he stood before. He had been embarrassed in front of his wife and daughter. He would never forget.

"Edgy, take my Henry and get up there in those rocks. Please, the rest of you stay at your seats by the fire. It will get chilly as the sun goes down. Get yourselves comfortable. I'm afraid that dinner will be delayed. Once those fellers out there pass, we'll take a little hike nearby and try to see if we can spy us a jackrabbit or coyote."

Those fellers, as Hank called them, didn't pass, at least right away they didn't. They rode right up into camp. Hank didn't recognize them at first.

Standing in front of them, blocking any further advance, Hank put on a friendly demeanor, his friendliest. But it was friendly without a smile. "Howdy, what can I do for you boys?"

The younger one to Hank's left responded, "Why we hoped you would be right hospitable. How about we join you for a spell and share a coffee?" His silent partner sported a sly smile as he began to dismount.

Hank did not like the look of the duo. He had honed his ability to size up people as a lawman in Laredo. It was a trait that had served him well.

"I wouldn't get off that saddle if I was you," Hank warned. The man stopped his motion, but still sported that ominous grin.

Hank now recognized them from their wanted posters. It was an old habit of his from his time as sheriff, checking into those wanted by the law. He never forgot a face. They both came into deadly focus now. No one but those two existed for him.

"That's not right friendly of you stranger. We've given you no cause to be inhospitable to fellow travelers," said the one on the left, also with an unnerving smile. "I see you have a real nice party with you. And a right pretty one, too," turning his head to leer at Elizabeth. "I'm sure they wouldn't mind some company."

The Franklins could sense the tension in the air, and all three trained their attention on what appeared to be a brewing confrontation.

"Well sir, *I* mind," said Hank, not at all friendly anymore. The warning was delivered with intentional force. He stood there, legs apart and balanced, right hand at his side with his holster tied low. The pair on horseback could not help but notice his stance. It said more than words. They didn't quite understand why the man standing before them had his hand in his left trouser pocket. They both passed it off as someone wanting to show casual confidence. Both had both stopped smiling by now.

"We seen that rifle a-poking out from them rocks a mile away mister. It don't scare us none. And you don't neither," said the talkative one.

Hank remained silent, waiting for their next move. He kept watch on their hands.

"Ok, partner. I'll lay it out for you," mister on the left said. "We aim to take what you got, including the girl. If'n you treat us right, we might just let you live. Tell whoever it is behind them rocks to come out with his hands in the air. Now unbuckle that gun belt of yours with that left hand you got dug in your pocket."

"Edgy, stay right where you are. Fix yourself on the quiet one. Now you two hear me this one time. I am willing to die to protect these folks. You have to ask yourselves if you are willing to die to rob them."

They hesitated before turning their horses around and slowly riding off. That talkative one though just had to have the last word. "We'll be seeing you again sometime. Real soon, I expect."

Hank didn't bother to respond. He didn't see the need, having delivered his message loud and clear. Although he was puzzled by the shovel sticking out of the quiet one's bedroll, Hank let that thought drop. He had practical matters to attend to and could not waste time on idle speculation. He watched them depart, not moving from his spot until they were safely away in the distance.

He called out, "Edgy it's safe to come on out now."

"I didn't sign on to your outfit to ride shotgun over it. I'm a cook, not a gunslinger. I couldn't hit an elephant at twenty paces."

"I know that, Edgy. But they didn't. Why don't you go on and start fixin' dinner."

The Franklins had been riveted to their seats until Hank finally turned around. The missus had earlier started to say something, but her husband had gently placed his hand on hers as a signal to wait. No longer able to contain herself, she unleashed her indignation, "Mr. Miller, what kind of an excursion are you running? You promised us a safe tour, not one in which we are threatened with our lives."

"Ma'am, I apologize. We haven't had any word of bandits in these parts for some time now. I keep in regular contact with the marshal in town and the Wells Fargo telegraph alerts. I would never have placed you folks in danger had I known anyone of their ilk had been anywhere nearby."

Now it was Mr. Franklin's turn. "It was your business to know. I demand we return to San Antonio this instant. And I want a refund. You'll be lucky I don't sue you," forgetting about the release form he signed before setting out. Mrs. Franklin nodded vigorously in agreement with her husband's sentiments.

Remaining calm in virtually all circumstances was a quality Hank had mastered. "Mister Franklin, Missus Franklin, it's way too dangerous to be traveling at night. Those two could be waiting to ambush us. There's plenty of places along the trail for them to hide and wait for us if they had a mind to. We wouldn't see them until we were filled with bullet holes. No, it's better to wait here until first light to set out. Me and Edgy will take turns keeping watch during the night. And don't worry, Mr. Franklin I was going to offer you a full refund in any case."

"I will take my turn at watch," Franklin responded and went back into the wagon, returning a moment later with his own *Colt New Line* in hand. It was a small revolver, relatively easy to conceal. "I no longer trust you to keep us safe. I will take responsibility for safeguarding my family."

Hank eyed that gun and the man who held it with suspicion. Before he could say anything else, Elizabeth found a way to call a truce.

"Mother, Father, I think Mr. Miller just saved our lives. Didn't you see him stand up to those men? He was willing to risk his own life to protect us."

That stymied her parents' coordinated attack. They would regroup later for another assault. For now though they were quiet.

Hank glanced her way, giving her a barely perceptible nod of thanks.

He now had a new worry. Jim and Tom were late. He saw no sign of them. What's worse, they had to reach the camp by the same route those outlaws were heading.

As a precaution Hank erected three tents and filled the bedrolls with sacks of supplies. In the dark an attacker would mistake them for a person sleeping soundly. The rice and beans would not mind the company of lead nearly as much as a human would. He had the Franklins sleep in the wagon. No attack came.

They awoke before dawn and quickly packed their equipment. Hank and Edgy had taken four-hour shifts a piece during the night to keep watch over the camp from the rocky outcropping overlooking it. True to his word, Mr. Franklin had taken a shift of his own. Hank stayed awake anyway, not quite trusting the skills of a lawyer from back East to spot danger in time.

The others had also slept little and were eager to be on their way. Despite the lack of sleep, all of them were too anxious to yet feel tired.

Hank had been careful not to stare into the fire during the night. He dared not risk the night blindness that had been fatal to the outlaws he had killed not so long ago.

"Are you sure it is safe to travel?" Mr. Franklin began. It was his version of a morning greeting. "Perhaps, you or your cook should ride ahead and bring back help."

Hank did not answer immediately. He was preoccupied with worry over his two friends who had failed to appear. "No, Mr. Franklin, it's best we stick together. If those outlaws are still out there waiting to ambush us, it would be easier for them to pick off a lone rider. We have greater safety in numbers."

"All right. I see the logic in that. One of the few times you have employed good sense during this entire fiasco."

Silent until now, Elizabeth asked, "Mr. Miller, you never told us who those men are. Do you know them?"

"Only by reputation, Miss."

"So you admit you know them?" Mrs. Franklin chimed in.

"Mother please. Let Mr. Miller finish."

"Well, yes I know *of* them, ma'am. As I said. Only by reputation." Her parents had apparently heeded their daughter's plea and waited, if impatiently, for the explanation.

"As I told you yesterday, I check the posters at the sheriff's office right regular. That's how I come to recognize them. That talkative one is Robert T. Coleman. I don't know what the 'T' stands for. I do know he's wanted for robbery and murder in the Oklahoma Territory. I guess he needs lots of range, like a bobcat, to do his hunting. That other one who never spoke is Arizona Bass. I guess he was named after the territory he was born in. He's wanted dead or alive for the same crimes as his partner. Like I told you, there was never any word they or anyone like them were out here in these parts."

What he didn't tell them was that Arizona was kin to the Bass brothers, a cousin of some kind. It's funny, he thought, that he should encounter yet another Bass gone bad. How many of these Basses were there? Was there a whole tribe of them somewhere? Did evil run in families? Could you inherit bad? And the past was always there, now come awake. Here was another real-life Bass, dogging his trail. If he could erase him from memory, would this latest Bass disappear? He knew that was pure fantasy but couldn't help thinking it. There was a part of his past that he wanted to forget and another he wanted to remember. But memory did not work that way he knew. Recollections could arise unbidden, triggered by the unlikeliest of events. And he sensed that Arizona Bass was not going away, despite any attempt to wish him gone.

Shrugging off those musings, he focused on the task at hand. "I think we should be on our way."

The three passengers boarded the wagon, the canvass now shielding them from the sun and maybe from bullets. Edgy snapped the reins. "Ho, get a move on fellas," he said as he nudged the horses forward. Hank led, riding on Charlie out front.

Two hours later he spotted them, two bodies lying on the road about two hundred yards ahead. Fear swept through him, not for himself, mind you, but for those two friends of his that never showed up. He scanned the area all around him. There was no cover for an ambush.

When they came upon the men, they halted. He rode to the back of the wagon and told the passengers, "It's best you folks stay inside."

Indignant, Mr. Franklin could not resist. "Why have we stopped? What's happening? I demand …"

Hank rarely lost his temper. But that man seemed bent on trying his patience. Hank cut him off. "Stay inside. All of you. Unless you want to see the bodies of my friends lying in the dirt."

Tom and Jim had never made it to the camp. They were to have played the role of bandits menacing their little party. Hank had told the Franklins in advance about the show they had prepared so they wouldn't be frightened.

Hank dismounted and hurried over to the two of them, laid out in the middle of the road. Blood had congealed in the dirt around them, the ground still moist.

Edgy climbed down and joined him. "Why do it like this? Why lay them out on the road? Those killers must be the meanest, cruelest critters I have ever come across."

Hank was thinking the same thing. He was also thinking of Julia and the kids. How was he going to break the news? His thoughts were broken by a stirring to his left, behind a collection of low brush. Must be a lizard he couldn't see. But some sense of his warned of danger. Then he heard a slightly muffled yell, "Now."

Up from the ground, behind those scrub bushes, a figure popped up, gun in hand. Without thinking, Hank, in his eerie focus, drew his Colt and fired. Whichever of the murderers he was, dropped backward into what became his shallow grave, never having had the opportunity to fire his weapon.

But behind him, from the road itself, the other of the two pulled the same trick. Rising from the ground he already had his pistol pointed at Hank.

Two shots rang out.

Part Two—Aftermath

Hank whirled and fired again. As he did, a second shot rang out. But it wasn't from the outlaw who stood suspended for a moment, two bullets having pierced his heart, one from in front and one from behind. A second later he collapsed to the ground.

Elizabeth stood there, immobile, right arm outstretched with pistol still in hand. It was as she had been taught. It was as she had practiced. "I may have attended a college founded by Quakers, Mr. Miller, but I am not one."

Their eyes locked. He would forever claim that hers had changed from bright blue to steel grey.

After he and Edgy had stood before their friends in silent prayer, Hank could not help but ask, "What possessed you to take your father's gun and leave the wagon, Miss Elizabeth?"

She appeared not at all shaken from the experience. That would come later. "I sensed you were in danger, Mr. Miller. I don't know where that came from. I honestly don't." What she did know, however, was that her destiny was now forever tied to this man.

They left the killers where they lay. People from town could take care of them later. Leave them for the coyotes for all Hank cared. They didn't even deserve burial on Boot Hill.

"Now I understand why one of them carried a shovel in his bedroll. Must have pulled that trick before. Worked on some poor souls. They were good at it. No one lived to spread word," Hank told Edgy. "They were likely hiding at Thompson's Bend. Spotted us before we could see them. Knew right when and where to dig their holes."

"It's downright unnatural to dig yourself a hole in the ground and cover yourself with a blanket, dirt on top. Well, it's a good thing they won't live to pull it again," the cook of all trades replied. "Dug their own graves this time, they did. Thanks to you. Good riddance to varmints."

Hank and Edgy carefully wrapped their friends in blankets and placed them in the wagon. Before leaving, Hank walked over to the first one he killed. "Mr. Colt may have said his pistols made all men equal. It's just that some men are more equal than others with that Colt of his in their hands." He spat on the dead man.

Then he went to the other, the one that both he and Elizabeth had shot. "I hope you like dwelling in that Valley of Death. I hear tell it's right warm down there." He spat again. Instead of carving two notches on the handle of his gun as a cold-blooded gunslinger might have done, Hank etched them on his brain. They were a reminder to thank whoever was watching over him so that he could protect others. When he reached his Appaloosa, Hank deftly swung himself into the saddle.

Mrs. Franklin was seated in front with the cook. Elizabeth and her father rode the spare horses. They spent the next few hours in silence.

Hank dropped them off at the Menger Hotel. He went to the marshal's office, told him what had happened, then brought Jim's and Tom's bodies to the morgue. He had one more task to perform.

He knocked on the door of the home. He heard her footsteps as Julia approached and opened it. "Oh, Hank. Thank goodness. I've been so worried."

Hank had his hat in his hand. "Julia, may I come in? I have some bad news." He had rehearsed what he was going to say. But the words still seemed to stick in his throat.

"Oh my God. It's Jim. Tell me he's safe. Please tell me that."

"Let's go in and sit."

She collapsed in a chair. "Two outlaws shot him and Tom. We got them bushwhackers, though." That was of little or no consolation to Julia.

The funeral was held the next day. The church overflowed with mourners, stretching out into the street. Family and friends, both Black and White attended. Hank was slated to give one of the eulogies. He was unsure of what he would say in front of so many people. He feared he would make a fool of himself and fail to provide comfort to Julia and her children.

He began, "James Handy was a good man. He was my friend." That was all he could manage before he broke down and started to cry. He shuttered with the sobs. That was comfort enough for those who had loved, still loved, a strong, skilled and uncompromisingly faithful human being.

Julia sat in the first pew with her three children next to her. She was dressed all in black, her face veiled. She had kept her composure, until then. She was a strong woman. Julia knew she would have to remain so for the sake of her youngsters.

In contrast, the burial of Tom Breakwater was a small affair. He had no local kinfolk and but a few friends. Hank, Edgy and the others respectfully listened as the preacher had his say. It took Hank a month to locate cousins in Missouri to notify them of Tom's passing.

The Franklins needed to wait three days to pack up and leave. Arranging for last minute unscheduled private railway cars was not an easy task. Hank came to see them off.

"I'm right sorry about the way things turned out," he said to them.

"We are too," Mr. Franklin stiffly replied, and with that he and his wife turned away to board the train.

"Mr. Miller," said Elizabeth, "Condolences on the death of your friends. Thank you for saving us."

"Thank you for saying that. I never meant to put you or your parents in peril."

"I know you didn't. I hope to one day see you again."

That last remark took him by surprise. He wondered if she really meant it.

She was the last to get on. Elizabeth started to walk away, but turned back to him and, for a brief instant, locked eyes once more with his. She gave him a wave and was gone.

The story of their harrowing escape took on a life of its own. Reporters flocked to San Antonio to write their own embellished accounts. Strangely enough, the notoriety only increased the volume of his business. Hank was fully booked for months in advance. He now held responsibility for a family, Jim's. He could not afford to let them down. Hank hired the town marshal and one of his deputies as role players. He had difficulty with that, replacing his friends. But he knew what he had to do to go on. Years later after he left and moved to San Francisco, he and Julia would continue to correspond. She would be sure to have him and Beth to dinner whenever they came back to town. Hank sent the first check to Julia in late April. It would be the first of many that would go to her and later to her children and her children's children.

***

He was sitting in his office when the letter arrived. His address on the envelope was written in ornate script. The color of the writing was a brilliant blue. Hank could not help but detect a vague but pleasant scent as he carefully opened it.

Philadelphia
June 3, 1890

Dear Mr. Miller,

I have decided to write in order to once again thank you for the good sense and bravery that you displayed throughout our time together. You saved our lives. I apologize for the way my parents treated you. I cannot fathom the depth of the grief you must feel at the loss of your friends. Please offer my sincerest condolences to their bereaved widows and families.

A version of our encounter with those outlaws was printed in *The New York World*. However, it did not come close to resembling the actual events.

Tell me of your business. I hope it was not harmed by the publicity.

Please give my regards to Edgy. Let him know we enjoyed his cooking. He possesses the skills of a fine chef.

I would greatly value your friendship and hope for a reply.

Sincerely,
Elizabeth Franklin

Hank did not know what to make of it. He had supposed he would never hear from her again. He tried to put Elizabeth out of his mind, but thoughts of her kept sneaking back in through some door he neglected to close. Maybe did not want to close.

For her part, Elizabeth had thought long and hard about what she would say. She had already decided upon the outcome. It was the journey she would have to properly navigate. She would have to shave a few rough edges and teach him to speak English. But that was about all that need be done. After all, she wouldn't want to change what she had found so attractive and admirable in the first place.

Hank did in fact reply. He worried that his writing would prove too primitive for such a refined young lady. But he persevered. He had the foresight to purchase *Webster's Dictionary* before embarking on a career of letters.

San Antonio, Texas
June 4, 1890

Dear Miss Elizabeth,

I was truly happy to hear from you. You have nothing to apologize for. None of it was your doing. And I have always wondered what might have happened if you had not been there to shoot that devil. Maybe I should be the one doing the thanking.

I will deliver your condolences. Jim Handy's wife, Julia, is a fine woman who now must raise her children alone. He owned part of the business, and she is due a share of the profits. Tom Breakwater has no close kin. I made right sure to send his last wages to his closest cousin in Missouri.

Edgy was glad that you remember him and grateful for your compliment about his cooking.

You asked about my business. It is doing fine. I guess the publicity from that tragedy did some good. I know that no other good has come of it, except maybe a friendship with you.

Your friend,
Hank Miller

They would exchange letters every few weeks from then on. Those missives gradually changed in tone. Miss Elizabeth gradually gave way to Dearest Beth with several stops in between. Her closing salutations progressed from Sincerely to Your Friend to Affectionately and finally to All My Love. It was precisely as she had planned, and he had dared to hope.

Early in December of 1891, Elizabeth told her parents over dinner, "Mr. Miller will be arriving by train tomorrow." She said it ever so casually without ever looking up from her meal.

"What on earth are you talking about Elizabeth? What Mr. Miller? Not *that* Mr. Miller. How do you know?" Her mother could do no more than stammer. She was horrified.

The implication was not lost on Mr. Franklin. "I forbid you to see that man."

"Father, he has come to ask you permission for my hand."

"Rubbish. I would sooner, sooner." He stopped himself from saying out loud what he thought: "... cut it off than yield it to that killer."

"Well, perhaps I should elope."

That stunned them. "You will not elope. That would scandalize us," her mother raised her voice, slamming her hand on the dark maple dining room table. But in those words the seeds of surrender had already been planted. Elopement no, the one viable alternative, wedding ceremony, yes.

Hank did indeed arrive the next day. As he descended from his *own* private car, Beth flew to him. No other word would suffice. Improper or not, they embraced. He lifted her off her feet and twirled her around. They kissed, the longest of their lives. Their bodies melded together. The letters, longer and longer over time, had made it seem as if they had been courting in person. And in their imaginations, they had.

Her parents stood, rigid and apart from them.

***

February 5, 1892: Elizabeth Louise Astor Franklin and Hank Samuel Miller.

Their wedding was a grand affair.

Chapter 13:
Nob Hill, San Francisco. June 19, 1906

(Six Years Earlier or Thereabouts. The Past)

An Ode

I t has taken me time to again set pen to paper. The terrible events of April eighteenth have prevented me from indulging in literary pursuits; that is, if one could elevate my poor scribbles to anything approaching the term literary. It seemed a frivolous and self-indulgent pursuit in times such as these.

But the time has now come to chronicle our relationship to the people and places of a community that has experienced devastating loss. I refer to this piece as an ode, rather than an elegy because I believe the city in which I live has not died. It is a living entity that will indeed, like the Phoenix, rise from its ashes. I believe that with all my heart. Beth and I will do whatever we can to contribute to its resurrection. I choose this date to write for a particular reason. Today is the fortieth anniversary of General Granger's Order to free all slaves in the state of Texas. It was not an idle gesture. He meant to see it done with force of arms, if necessary. He desired to rebuild society. With the same resolve I will see this city rebuilt to surpass even its former grandeur. Galveston accomplished it a few years after the Great Storm of 1900 washed the entire city away. We are not Pompeii, forever buried in ash. We are not.

Beth and I first came to San Francisco in 1892, during our honeymoon. We had decided to spend it in California, never having visited the state. It took almost a week to reach the west coast. We traveled from Philadelphia by private railway car. The journey was a blur. To tell the truth I honestly cannot recall the scenery of the vast country we crossed. We hadn't spent much time watching it.

Our first stop was The Raymond in South Pasadena. It was a marvel atop Beacon Hill. The views of the surrounding countryside were stunning. Nothing, however, rivaled the stunning views offered by my bride.

We took the hotel's horse drawn carriage, the *Tally Ho*, into Los Angeles proper for a tour on a single occasion. The City of Angels, as it is called, was a bit of a disappointment though. There was little of interest to do or see. The oil wells that dotted the landscape emitted a foul odor that permeated the air in parts of the town and its namesake county.

One week later we were off to San Francisco. We stopped overnight in Monterey, up the coast and between the two cities. The town itself was struggling but the Hotel Del Monte was a pleasant surprise. The cliffs overlooking the

Pacific were nothing short of spectacular. Then it was on to the City by the Bay.

I pause here because I did not intend this essay to be a travelogue or an advertisement for hotels. From the time of my earliest writings I have been given to stray into paths of irritating digression. I must learn to constrain myself. Fortunately, Beth seems to find these side trips diverting.

We arrived in the early morning hours, fog blanketing the bay. The sun would burn it off, as it did every day, before noon. There was a chill in the crisp July air, a fact much re-marked upon by visitors and writers alike. In fact, Mr. Twain, never short on wit, is reported to have commented that the coldest winter he ever spent was summer in San Francisco. We didn't mind at all. We found the climate bracing.

We stayed in the Palace Hotel, now tragically laying in ruins. It was a sight to behold when we first arrived and in a perfect location to begin our explorations. This is the final time I will mention a hotel and beg the indulgence of the reader (Beth) for its mention. I merely wanted to adhere to historical accuracy.

I believe our most enjoyable outing was to Sausalito, a picturesque town by the ocean. I was fascinated by the sea, having spent my formative years well inland. It wasn't until my thirty-third year that I discovered the Pacific. Even Beth, who had traveled the civilized world, had never seen its like. We were mesmerized by the magnificence of the coast, from the cliffs and bays to the quiet beaches and inlets. Having be-come entranced by the city and its nearby ocean, we decided this was where we would settle and establish the headquarters for our company. We took Mr. Greeley's advice and went about as far west as the continent would allow.

We would keep the office in San Antonio, ably patrolled by the former marshal of the town and a staff of tour guides and cowboys turned actors, including Edgy. We would come back to visit periodically. Our auditors always preceded us. It was the heart of our business in its earliest days, and we bore the responsibility of oversight. The visits always included dinner with Julia and those of her children who had yet to spring the coop.

But San Francisco of 1893 was a rapidly expanding municipality whose possibilities attracted entrepreneurs of all stripes, including us. We rented an office downtown, until we could find suitable permanent accommodations for our business. We remained in a suite in the establishment where we had temporarily but happily parked our lives, The Palace (Don't judge me too harshly, Beth, for mentioning a hotel again.) It was the place the twins first called home. They didn't have the patience to wait until our residence on Nob Hill could be completed before making their grand entrance into the world. The staff and guests were captivated by them.

This leads me to the present, thirteen years after our arrival in a city which deserves better fortune than it has lately encountered. To be entirely accurate it is the people of this city that deserve better. However, as I have often observed, Fate can be a cruel mistress. Did Carthage and its residents deserve its utter destruction? Did Herculaneum? Did my friends, Charlie, Tom, or Jim?

How quickly things can change. Beth and I had taken the children to see the great Enrico Caruso perform at the

Mission Opera House the night before the world seemed to end. We had gone from the most sublime voice nature had ever endowed to the most vicious event nature could conjure in the space of a few hours.

Was it Fate that left us untouched while others perished? What in fact does the word actually mean? Is one's life pre-determined and our choices mere illusion? Perhaps, it is part of the great Deity's impenetrable plan. Or are we like the microscopic particles described by Robert Brown that randomly interact with one another? Fate, I think, has many meanings and is an artificial construct of man to explain the events he cannot otherwise comprehend.

And what of devastation and renewal. These terms surely describe realities. But they too can be metaphorical. Miss Dickinson eloquently put it this way:

> She died—this was the way she died;
> And when her breath was done,
> Took up her simple wardrobe
> And started for the sun.
> Her little figure at the gate
> The angels must have spied,
> Since I could never find her
> Upon the mortal side.

Interpret the poem as you will, as metaphor for the reality of renewal or comment about the afterlife or both.

Our city is due an afterlife.

We have done our best to speed that along. So many were displaced by the fire that followed the earth's convulsion that a tent city was established at the Presidio. A testament to American efficiency and generosity, the Army quickly moved in to provide order and relief aid to the hundreds of thousands in need of shelter and food. Even the Navy contributed, lending the U.S.S. *Chicago*, enabling the evacuation of a huge number of residents. And as always, Clara Barton's Red Cross was there to render whatever aid it could.

Beth and I established the San Francisco Relief Agency as well as the City Relief Fund. Once the Army declared it safe from fire, we set up a food distribution center on Market and Broad, adjacent to our office, which had somehow been spared. We took in our employees, all of whom had survived the earthquake and subsequent fire. The area around down-town looked as if it had been attacked by a marauding horde, armed with cannon and fury.

Our home was also spared as were most of the structures of Nob Hill. Our well healed neighbors were generally grate-ful for their own good fortune. The heirs to the one-time California Senator Leland Stanford, railroad magnate and robber baron, worked tirelessly on behalf of the needy. They lived in that great mansion of theirs, not more than a ten-minute walk from our own home.

As a practical matter the work of rebuilding will require funding. We will provide what we can. The renewal of this great city will not happen on its own. Beth and I are already forming a Reconstruction Committee and are to meet with Mr. Giannini to discuss the necessary financing. His Bank of America has the reputation of being a reputable institution, a lender willing to take a chance on a person without the backing of traditional collateral. For Mr. Giannini, the only assets a person needs to secure a loan are honesty, character and vision. I cannot think of any period in my lifetime when the work of civic engagement was more required than at this moment.

Those of us who have the means are tasked with a special responsibility. Our entire family understands the burden that has been placed upon us. We will do our part.

I reflect on the events of these last weeks and ask myself the same questions I have been asking for years. Why was I again permitted to remain unscathed? Why was my family allowed the same privilege? Did my luck rub off on them? I will have to have a conversation with Rabbi Voorsanger when, G-d willing, we can find the time to spare away for the work at hand. I have always been lucky, G-d knows. Or was this mere Brownian motion?

Chapter 14:
San Francisco. April 18, 1906

(Six Years Earlier or Thereabouts. The Past)

The Earth Trembles

The earth shook. It shook so violently it was as if it wanted to shake off man and all his works. The source of that discontent was a tectonic shift of immense proportion.

The earthquake struck at 5:13 AM on the morning of April 18, 1906, a Wednesday. Its bone jarring effects would be felt at least as far as Eureka, about two hundred seventy miles to the north, and Salinas, well over one hundred miles to the south. Although aftershocks were few, they occurred in the Imperial Valley and may have even angered the fracture beneath distant Santa Monica Bay.

Beth and Hank were abruptly awakened from sleep by the wrath of the San Andreas fault. At first, they had no idea what was happening. The children ran into the room. They were as frightened as the adults. "Earthquake," erupted from a place somewhere deep inside that Hank did not know existed. The shaking went on for less than two minutes in separate spurts but felt much longer to those caught up in it.

They gave each of their two thirteen-year-old twins and eleven-year-old daughter brief hugs and told them to get dressed quickly. The word quickly was unnecessary. They were already running down the hall back to their rooms.

As the sun rose moments later, they could see the devastation in the city below. Much of downtown was shrouded in fog and dust, but the remains of many structures were still visible. The taller buildings peaked above the haze. A cloud of smoke would soon begin to engulf the city as fires broke out everywhere. Those fires would be attributed to exploding gas lines. As they watched helplessly, the Millers would see an occasional plume of fire and smoke with its accompanying boom, signaling yet another explosion to add to the city's misery. It turned out that many blazes were set by the property owners themselves because their insurance covered fire but not earthquake. Whatever the cause of the conflagration, it was said to account for eighty to ninety percent of the refugees that numbered in the hundreds of thousands. The scale of the disaster was unimaginable.

The five of them sat and stared until the clouds of dust and smoke reached them. They had been mesmerized in the way that disaster can capture attention. Last night's recital seemed a universe away. They wondered what might have happened to the world's leading tenor whose reception they had attended after the concert. Enrico Caruso had been staying at the Plaza, now utterly destroyed. They had even personally toasted him, the children each allowed a half flute of champagne for the occasion.

Hours later, they finally went inside. Beth tried calling the office, but the telephone line emitted an eerie howl. It was a scream for help from a dying city. They had no idea how their employees fared.

Nob Hill was an oasis of safety. Few of the upper-class homes and estates had even been damaged. Leland Stanford's mansion lay untouched not a half mile away. Even that ancient vase, which stood guard in the Millers' foyer, escaped damage. It had teetered but not fallen. Beth vowed to better secure it, which is exactly what she did later that day.

Fortunately, all three workers and their families from the tour company made it up to the Miller's by late afternoon. They were smart enough to seek the safety of a section of the city that appeared relatively intact; and it was where their employers lived. These refugees from the broken city would stay at the mansion for the next seven months until appropriate living quarters could be found for them. Afterall, the Millers, the Lord knew, had enough room and, more importantly, possessed an immense generosity of spirit. Hank in particular always felt grateful for deliverance from hardscrabble times. He could no longer thank all the people who had helped him along the way. But he certainly could lend a hand to those who needed it. From what he could see a whole lot of people would need that hand. However, neither he nor Beth yet knew how many that would be.

Days later, when the magnitude of the devastation became clear, they would be among the first to chart the course for the recovery.

Chapter 15:
Nob Hill, San Francisco. June 20, 1912

(The Present)

The Burden of Memory

Before he departed on his journey to Morocco, Hank left three letters, one for Beth, one for Rachael and one for the boys. He knew the terrible danger he faced and the peril in which he placed the twins. Too many things had to go near perfectly for their ruse to succeed. He was counting on his luck to see them though. He was counting on the meticulous planning to which they all had contributed to get them out alive. He was also counting on his own finely honed survival skills.

Letter One—Rachael

My Dearest Rachael,

I know you wanted to come with us. But I knew it would be the wrong decision. I write this letter to explain. You are a young woman already of formidable means and character. You are smart beyond words and beautiful beyond imagining. You possess an emotional resonance, the ability to sense the feelings of others. I coined a word, translated from the Greek, to describe this admirable trait of yours. I call it empathy. And you can shoot like the dickens. However, none of those traits, as admirable as they are, qualify you to accompany me and your brothers on our expedition. It goes without saying that what we are doing is dangerous. That is precisely the reason you cannot come. But not why you think. Someone must remain behind to comfort your mother, should the unimaginable happen. That someone is you.

Our president, Teddy Roosevelt, said it best. "Nobody knows how much you know, until they know how much you care." You know so much and care so much, so much like your mother. The very traits that qualify you to come with us are the very ones that best qualify you to be the one to stay behind.

My charge to you is to grow strong, learn much, marry well, and have a passel of children. Take care of your mother. I fully expect to return with the boys and me intact. I will do my best to do that, G-d willing. I pledge that on a father's honor.

I shall love you forever and always,
Papa

Letter Two—BenDavid

My Dearest Twins,

You two were the sweetest of boys and have grown into the strongest of men. I couldn't be more proud of you both. I write this letter as a confession of sorts. I am guilty of having placed you in inestimable danger. If anything has happened to either of you, I will never forgive myself. Neither would your mother ever forgive me, alive or dead. The honest truth is I needed you at my side. Selfish, I know. But I didn't think this impossible rescue could succeed without you. I pray that it has.

I do not want to sing your praises overmuch. You both are already too full of yourselves. I admit, though, that your pride is well earned, well, most of the time.

I charge you with the same responsibilities I gave Rachael. Grow strong, learn much, marry well, and have a passel of children. Take care of your mother. I had fully expected to return with the two of you and me intact, having secured the freedom of Ali and Amina. I will have done my best to do that, G-d willing. I pledged that on a father's honor.

If, however, I failed to protect you both and one of you has not returned, I pray you would have it in your heart to forgive me.

I shall love you forever and always,
Pops

Letter Three—Beth

My Dearest Beth,

I know you didn't want me to go. I know that you wanted to go with me. I know you know why that wasn't possible: Rachael. I know you know that I love you with all my heart. I owe you everything good in my life. In fact, I owe you my life. I can now finally admit that it was your bullet that first pierced that man's evil heart. Mine was but an afterthought.

Having made that concession, I feel less guilty in placing the burden of memory on you in the same way a wise and kind elderly woman once placed it on me. If I should not return, it must be you that passes along the stories of all who came before. They must survive in the memories of those who benefited from their presence on this earth. It is a way of keeping them alive of course. But it is also a way to pass down wisdom to our descendants so that they may be the inheritors of the insights and love of generations past.

I started my very first essay that you assigned to me with this sentence, "I've done a lot of things in my life that I'm not right proud of." It remains true to this day. When sharing the essence of a life the trick is to tell all the parts of it which matter to the future. The pitfalls to avoid. The traits to emulate. You know the stories that must be told. I trust you with all my being to do so. You will tell our children and grandchildren those stories. And you will charge them with the very same obligation I have placed upon you, the burden of memory.

I ask for no physical shrine for the people who have helped us along the way, only that they be stored somewhere in the brain where memories live, to be consulted as the need arises.

Do you remember when you asked me why I carried that old locket of Charlie's in my left pocket that contained a picture of a woman I had never met? I told you it was because I had to keep my gun hand free. It was a flippant answer, not one at all really. We left it at that.

I admit to you now that I never told you I gripped it tight when I first saw you set down from that train in San Antonio. What a sight to behold you were! I hold on to it whenever I sense danger. And what a danger you were! That keepsake is more than a lucky charm. It is a way to honor his memory. It is a reminder of a man who taught me how to be good and how to stay that way.

It is said that memory begets (In truth I said it.). It can give birth to all varieties of emotion. It can set off alaurms at the most inopportune of times and keep you a-twistin' and a-turnin' all night long. It can also set off the alarms that save your life. It can comfort or disturb. I can only hope that your memory of me does more of the former than the latter.

Honey, I aim to return alive, and to return my sons in the same condition in which they left. We will come back safe and sound, G-d willing. I know that I rely on luck to see me through. I learned long ago, however, that it has been more than luck that has been at work. There's Providence, the sense that someone above has been protecting me in order that I can protect others. But there's something else I have come to realize. I never told anyone what I said to that dead bushwhacker lying on the road: "Mr. Colt may have said his pistols made all men equal. It's just that some men are more equal than others with that Colt of his in their hands." If you hadn't already surmised, that more equal man with the Colt is me.

Little gal that you are, think of me with a smile on your face. I aim to see that smile and those eyes of brilliant blue (not the steel grey ones) once again.

With All My Love,
Me

P.S. Let's take us a tumble when I return!

Chapter 16:
San Antonio, Texas, May 18, 1891
Zinat, Morocco, September 14, 1891

(Twenty-one Years Earlier or Thereabouts. The Past)

First Rescue and Riches

P eople would often wonder where Hank got the money to start his business. Or how he and Elizabeth were so quickly able to open offices in so many major cities. Or how they were able to afford that magnificent mansion of theirs on Nob Hill. They often assumed that the funds came from Beth's wealthy parents. They would be wrong.

It was noon when Hank returned to his office from one of his patented tours, having entertained a politically connected family from Washington, D.C. It had gone well, the children delighted by the actors playing the desperados Hank faced down. No bullets were ever exchanged in those contrived encounters. And the parents enjoyed the historical narrative about the Alamo. They never knew it was a romanticized version. They had all been transfixed by tales of the bandits that had once roamed the countryside, occasionally coming to town to rob a bank. In Hank's telling the posse always caught up with them. He had adopted the advice from a local newspaperman who had told him, "This here is Texas son. When legend comes into conflict with truth, print the legend. It sells papers." Hank spun his yarns and sold his tours.

As he went through the mail that had accumulated while he was away, he came across an opened envelope at the top of the stack. It had enough stamps on it to weigh down a pack mule. His full-time secretary, Martha Albright, had placed the correspondence in what she deemed the order of importance. This one was addressed to Mr. H. Miller, American West Tour Company, San Antonio, Texas, United States of America. It intrigued him. So, it was the first one he opened.

Tangier, Morocco
April 5, 1891

Dear Mr. Miller,

I am writing to schedule a tour of your wild West. I have always wanted to see it first-hand. I have read so much about it. Your reputation has reached the far edges of the world, thanks to the series in *The New York World*. When I inquired about your reputation, a British officer by the name of Col. Figgins commended your company to me. He is training my troops at my villa outside of Tangier.

Tell me, have you had the acquaintance of Wyatt Earp or Bat Masterson? Have you ever been to the OK Corral?

I am more than willing to pay whatever fee you require. In fact, I insist on paying at the very least double your customary charges. I will be traveling with two of my wives and their attendants. Two servants and a guard will accompany me. I will have a considerable amount of baggage.

Wire instructions for payment to my factotum, Ayoub al-Mansour, Tangier, Morocco.

Respectfully,
The Hon. Hasan Al-Aziz

Hank was astonished that his fame had reached Morocco, wherever that was. He had never heard of the place before. He assumed it was a country in the Middle East somewhere, based on the name of the person who had signed the missive, and that Tangier was a city from the way the letter had been headed. He had absolutely no idea who on earth Col. Figgins was. He would, however, remember that name when it came up again a few years later. What he did know was that he was offered twice his usual charges. He would need it to cover the expenses to take care of that many clients. In fact, he would have to rent a veritable wagon train and the supplies that went along with it.

He wired back instructions for payment and sent a letter with advice about train travel, accommodations, and gear. Hank had become a full-service travel agent. He offered to make all the arrangements. And that is precisely what his secretary, Mrs. Albright, did. For an additional fee, of course.

***

Hasan Al-Aziz arrived on the twenty fourth of July with his entire retinue. As always Hank was there at the train station to meet his guests. This time, however, he came armed with three wagons and a buggy with two rows of seats. He had read about Morocco and Islam in the *Encyclopedia Britannica* that Jane had willed to him, but did not know the seating etiquette regarding multiple wives.

The bodyguard was the first to set down from the train. He was tall, well built and dressed in traditional Moroccan garb, flowing white trousers and blouse. The armed escort wore a wide black belt at the waist that held a holstered British Webley Revolver and a sheath containing a jambiya. He looked to the right and left before stepping to the side to allow his charges to descend. Hank recognized competence when he saw it. This man would be a dangerous adversary. He had no desire to find out just how dangerous.

The Honorable Hasan Al-Aziz appeared in the doorway next, paused to wait for a nod from his guard and then came down the metal steps to the station floor. He was resplendent in cream colored djellaba trimmed in gold thread worn over his light tan suit. That suit, among many others he owned, had been imported from Harrods of London. A brown tarboosh stood proudly atop his white head of hair. Al-Aziz was no more than five-and-a-half feet tall, but his elegant dress and air of casual authority made him appear taller. It was the hat that had caught Hank's eye. It had no practical use. "That hat won't keep a single ray of Texas grade sun off that man's head," he thought. "It does look a-might fashionable though." Little did he know that the fez, as it was popularly known, had become the rage among the gentlemen of Europe. And contrary to popular legend, the Ottomans had appropriated it from Morocco and not the other way around.

Hank, ten feet away and unsure of his next move, waited for some sign that it was safe to approach. He reckoned that any sudden move, even an innocent one, would be unwise.

Al-Aziz simply walked up to him, smiling broadly. "Mr. Hank Miller, it is a true honor to meet you."

"The honor, sir, is all mine."

"This is Ali," he said, pointing to his bodyguard. "I trust him with my life."

"Well, sir, we'll make sure we give him no call to have your trust in him worried none. Our excursion will be as safe as a baby in its momma's arms." Hank was playing his role now, exaggerating his West Texas.

The rest of the entourage followed. Al-Aziz sat in the front with Hank. Ali, ever vigilant, took a seat in the second row. The two wives, both veiled and as yet to be introduced, boarded the covered wagon with their female attendants. The two other servants remained behind to load the baggage onto the other wagons with Edgy himself to help in the effort to bring it all to the hotel.

On the morning of departure, the tribal leader had his servants line up in front of the first wagon to introduce them to Hank, Edgy and the other driver, a former deputy, Frank González. Each of his retainers stepped forward as he called out their names and slightly bowed their heads in stately fashion.

Al-Aziz had spent five years in England. His father had sent him to Cambridge and then on to The London School of Economics as preparation for eventually taking over management of the family fortune. He always recalled his days there with great fondness, especially the ladies whose hearts he had broken. Al-Aziz had adopted the mannerisms and weapons of the nation of his affection while still retaining Moroccan traditions. He blended the two cultures as his style of dress attested. It was the British he chose to emulate, if in limited fashion. But, most of all, he was a Moroccan patriot, devoted to the sultan. Al-Aziz detested the French, Spanish, and Germans who seemed bent on appropriating his country.

Before leaving, Hank made absolutely sure that Mr. Al-Aziz and Ali, especially Ali, knew that two cowboy actors, playing the role of desperados, would show up the next morning. Hank would shoo them away. To be sure, he reminded them of the upcoming entertainment while they made camp late that afternoon. Ali had always seemed to keep an Enfield slung on his shoulder, his pistol and curved knife easily accessible on his belt. Hank wanted no misunderstandings.

Undeterred by Hank's effort at reassurance, as soon as he saw those riders approaching, Ali undid the strap holding his gun in its holster. He held his rifle at the ready during the entire feigned confrontation. He almost relaxed when they rode out of sight.

It was not until the second night in the Hill Country that Al-Aziz took Hank aside to introduce his wives, Alia and Yasmin. The two were much younger than their husband and quite beautiful. They had remained apart from the others at camp and would remain so for the rest of the sojourn. As they strolled back to their separate fire and were out of earshot, Al-Aziz said to Hank, "Keeps one young, you know, younger wives. I have one more at home." He had a big grin on his face as he spoke.

Suddenly his countenance turned serious. "Did you really kill all those men that the newspapers claimed? They made it seem that you left the entire West strewn with bodies." This fearsome reputation did not seem to match the kind and well-mannered man with whom he had become acquainted.

"Well sir, I never did read anything of those accounts. I don't rightly know what they had to say about me. I wouldn't set much store in those stories of theirs. I can tell you that I shot seven men, one with the help of a lady. To this day I don't know which of our bullets actually did the job. All of them were downright killers and bushwhackers. I started out seeking vengeance and wound up dispensing justice. I began my life wanting to kill no one. I want it to end that way. Each life is sacred with the exception of some polecats now in their graves and some that oughta be. I take no pleasure in killing."

Al-Aziz was impressed. So impressed, in fact, that he would change the course of Hank's life. The Moroccan chieftain and his entourage set off for home on the thirty-first of July. "Thank you, Mr. Al-Aziz. It has truly been a pleasure. Now, I may say that to all my guests. I admit I don't always mean it. This time I do. I truly do."

They shook hands; but before he departed, Al-Aziz gave Hank a packet. "Open it, my friend, when you return to your office." With that cryptic remark he turned and was off.

Ali nodded in Hank's direction, a smile crossing his face. It was the first time Hank had seen the man smile. And then, he too was off, climbing aboard the train ahead of his charges to clear away any potential threat.

Hank was anxious to open the parcel. He briefly greeted Martha as he entered. She was busy at her desk, attending to business. He really wanted to get at that mysterious package. Hank used his pocketknife to cut the cord that encircled it and tore off the brown paper wrapping. Inside was a soft leather pouch ten by twelve inches. In it, Hank saw wads of cash. He turned it upside down. A piece of paper, the money and a small box tumbled onto his desk. He picked up the paper first. It was a letter, written on fine grade material.

Letters, letters. He started thinking of those he had been exchanging with Beth. They had become a rather big part of his life. So had letters become essential to his business. He broke from the brief Elizabeth inspired daydream and began to read.

My Dear Hank,

I have greatly enjoyed your hospitality. Now you must enjoy mine. Enclosed you will find a sufficient sum to book passage to my home in Zinat. I trust you have the means to make those arrangements yourself. Wire your itinerary to Ayoub al-Mansour, Tangier, Morocco. He will have someone meet you at the dock. In no circumstance are you to go to a hotel on your own. Do not be concerned. We will take all precautions necessary to ensure your safety.

With Kindest Regards,
H. Al-Aziz

He then opened the small, carved wooden box. There sat a rose-colored diamond nestled in satin, exquisitely cut in a pentagonal shape.

Hank was not sure what to make of it. That man seemed cocksure he would come to his home in some faraway country. Who knew how long that trip would take? He couldn't leave his business unattended. He couldn't suddenly cancel reservations to go off gallivanting. Or could he? Marshal Johns and Martha were capable of supervising the business in his absence. Mr. Al-Aziz had left him more than enough money to get him there. And then there was the matter of that gem.

"Martha," he called, "I have a job for you."

Hank sat down and wrote a letter to Beth, explaining his intention to go to Morocco. He desperately wanted her to understand that he might be able to secure their financial future. Another jewel like the one in the box would be just the ticket. What he didn't say was that he relished the thought of one last adventure in a faraway land.

Hasan Al-Aziz, for his part, didn't say certain things either. He didn't say he had a daughter to marry off to a man he admired. He didn't say why that diamond had been cut as a five-sided figure. It was not by chance that five was the number of the Pillars of Islam. Hank would need to convert before even a betrothal could take place. And he didn't say that above all else, he would have to teach Hank to speak the King's English.

***

Landlubber that he was, Hank remained in his cabin for the first two days of the voyage to England. The seasickness had taken a hold of him and what a hold it had. It would take that time to gain his sea legs. Fortunately, the rest of his trip, all the way to Morocco, was quite pleasant. Little did he know then that he would one day retrace his entire journey.

Two weeks later, Hank walked down the ramp of the steamship at the passenger docks in Tangier. He spotted the driver of the carriage waiting for him holding a large placard that read, *Mr. Miller*. Standing next to the conveyance was Ali.

They dropped him off at the Hotel Continental, a place to which he would return years later, under circumstances much less auspicious.

Before he stepped down from the carriage, Ali placed a hand on his arm, "Mr. Miller, do not leave your hotel. There are those who would kidnap you and hold you for ransom." It was the first time Ali had actually spoken to him. In a way Hank wished he hadn't. What on earth had he gotten himself into?

"I will be back at nine in the morning to pick you up if that is acceptable to you." He noticed the look of concern on his charge's face and added, "Don't be overly alarmed. As long as you remain inside you will be perfectly safe."

However, Hank *was* alarmed. As soon as he got to his room the first thing he did was unpack his Henry and his Colt.

True to his word, Ali and his driver were waiting for Hank as he emerged from the hotel entrance the next day at the appointed hour.

"Good morning, Mr. Miller. I trust you slept well."

Hank had not.

"The journey to Zinat will take about a week. Our horses and supplies await us at the stables of Mr. Al-Aziz on the eastern outskirts of the city. We will be there in about two hours. Do not worry about your safety. You are under the protection of a man honored by all, including the brigands who might otherwise threaten you. Even Raisuli would not dare to harm you. He and Mr. Al-Aziz are allies in their hatred of the Europeans that infest our country."

"I thank you for that bit of comfort. I think I will still keep my six shooter at the ready, if you don't mind. And by the way, please call me Hank."

"I don't mind at all. You are the guest of a great man and may do as you please. I hope to one day try out that famous pistol of yours and the Henry."

"Why that would be my pleasure, Ali. But only under one condition."

"What is that, sir, ah, Hank?"

"That I get the chance to do the same with your Webley and Enfield."

"Of course. We will have ample opportunity for target practice."

They set off for the stables. Hank had envisioned them to be simple wooden structures as was the custom in the West. What he found was a grand villa on a hill overlooking a green valley to the east and Tangier to the west. The compound was surrounded by a wall of white stone at least ten feet high and thicker than a bison in summer. The main house was a grand two-story building. A curved balcony supported by five pillars stood at the entrance.

A stallion was awaiting him in its stall. Hank marveled at its beauty, white and dappled grey. It was magnificent, but still not his Charlie. A stable hand led the horse out and saddled him. Hank adjusted the stirrups to his liking and hoisted himself aboard. He cantered to the caravan that was forming.

And what a caravan it was! He counted no less than fourteen mules, heavily laden with cargo led by drivers and a bunch more with riders atop. There were at least twelve armed guards, all bearded, in uniforms of traditional flowing light tan trousers and matching shirt. They wore a short navy-blue jacket with brass buttons over it. Their brown leather sandals were designed for both style and durability. They all carried rifles crosswise on their backs and curved scabbards housing a sword on their belts. The outfits and equipment reflected Al-Aziz's inclinations, a blend of Moroccan and British, the latter being the lone exception to his distaste of Europeans.

Hank wondered why a man as powerful and, frankly, as intimidating as Al-Aziz would need a heavily armed escort to safeguard his caravan. Sensing his thoughts, Ali explained, "Mr. Al-Aziz is a careful man. Even though he is of great stature, a party bearing items of great value would be a

temptation that a roving band of brigands could not resist."
He flashed a broad smile. "Do not worry. We will keep you
safe."

"I place myself in your hands, Ali. It's also why I carry
my own six gun," he said as he patted his Colt.

Five days later they arrived at Zinat. The closer they
came, the more Hank realized the enormity of the place. It
was a fortress. A high stone wall surrounded a Moorish style
palace. Guards in the same uniform as those with whom he
traveled patrolled along its top. The outbuildings were the
color of stone, presumably to ward off the relentless heat of
the sun.

"Impressive, is it not?" said Ali as they were about to
pass through the massive wooden gates that marked the entrance to the compound.

Hank was indeed impressed. He had never seen its like
before. The villa outside of Tangier could easily fit inside this
palace several times over. He and Ali parted ways with the
caravan and headed to the steps leading to the grand edifice.
A line of date palms stood as welcoming sentinels over the
grounds in front of the enormous structure. Flowering plants
of varieties unknown to Hank lined the pathway up to the
elaborately carved palace doors, gold filigree reflecting the
sun.

"Forgive me Hank. I almost forgot. Please remove your
gun belt. None but members of the private guard may enter
the palace with weapons. Of course, your Colt will be well
cared for and returned to you when you leave." He did as he
was told and handed it to Ali.

Two servants stood at the ready and opened each of the doors outward. Hank noticed the immediate drop in temperature as he stepped inside. A retainer was there to greet them. He addressed only Hank. "Welcome, Mr. Miller. I am Karim, majordomo of the household, head butler if you will. On behalf of the Honorable Hasan Al-Aziz, I welcome you to his abode. We have prepared refreshments for you and a bath. You may choose which you prefer first. Mr. Al-Aziz will join you later." He nodded to Ali who retreated to the doorway.

"I will see you later, Mr. Miller." He knew that the formal means of address was required in the presence of Karim. Hank winked at him in reply.

Hank was mesmerized. A great staircase stood twenty yards in front of him. It seemed to rise to the heavens. The floor was black marble with intricate designs in gold, blue, and tan. It was polished to a high sheen. Vases and potted plants were everywhere to be seen. It was unlike anything he could have imagined, and this was merely the threshold to the treasures that lay within.

"I think I should make myself presentable and take that bath first."

He followed Karim in a daze of sorts, gawking, at the surroundings. Gawking, no other word would adequately capture his wonder. He was a tourist in a house of wealth beyond imagination. When he reached his chambers, his escort clapped twice. Six women, holding vessels of steaming water, appeared out of what seemed thin air. They carried three brass containers with side handles, each held by one of the servants. Others brought in his luggage. He hardly noticed.

Hank took in the intricately laid mosaic tile flooring and the rugs imported from Persia that covered the walls. No portraits of people hung anywhere. The bed was a four poster with an elaborate canopy. Karim led him to a second room where a bath of pink marble was set into the floor. The women poured the contents of the containers into it. They left immediately after completing their task.

"I will leave you to it, Mr. Miller. If you want refreshments brought to your room, or anything at all, pull on the rope by your bed." He turned and left.

Hank was left standing there in amazement.

Later that evening, Karim returned to escort him to dinner. There he joined his host, three wives, and youngest daughter. Al-Aziz popped out of his seat and embraced Hank. "Ah, my friend, I am so glad that you accepted my invitation. I apologize for not greeting you in person. Alas, the exigencies of business. Let me introduce you to my wives. You have already met Alia and Yasmin. This is Hanan, my third." He paused for a moment and continued. "And this is Jasmina, my youngest daughter."

Hank replied, "It is a real pleasure to meet you ladies. You are all as pretty as a red rose in full bloom." He took the seat offered him at the opposite end of the dinner table. He was so distant from his host that he felt as if he were looking at him through the wrong end of a spyglass.

"You may be wondering how my family accumulated all this enormous wealth."

It was exactly what Hank was thinking.

"I am embarrassed to say, my distant ancestors were pirates and brigands, but pirates and brigands of the first order.

They raided the trade routes at sea and on land from Spain across the Mediterranean and into Africa. Even to Persia and the legendary silk road. You can imagine the riches. Our family tells the story that our forebears may have started out as thieves and cutthroats, but found it far more profitable to exact tribute. And far safer. Why risk one's life to steal when extracting treasure from others could be done in a much more civilized manner, eh? The great Banafsaj ibn Abi Talib, may he dwell in heaven's peace, used the wealth accumulated over the centuries to build this very palace in 1713. He purchased respectability. And he continued the illegal activities on the side, even after investing in his own trade caravans. We are the beneficiaries, you see, of a checkered past. My father, Abdel Al-Aziz Rahim, may he dwell in heaven, invested wisely as did I. You see the result all around you. We have become legitimate, but soft, I assure you, we are not."

The food was magnificently presented. Hank had never had such an elaborately prepared meal, not even at Jim and Julia's. At the end he was so stuffed, he could barely get out of his seat. "Let's take a stroll," Aziz offered. Hank wasn't sure he could do it, but he dutifully obeyed.

They walked to the atrium. It was a botanic garden with an elaborate glass enclosure overhead. It even had its own lily pond. The orchids were spectacular. "I have a botanist in residence, you know. He comes from England, of course, and lives here six months out of the year. He is getting up in age, though. I do not know how much longer he will be able to tolerate the hardships of the journey back and forth. I suspect from your detailed narrative during our tour about your native flora that you have an interest in botany. Perhaps I could sponsor your further education in that field. Mr. Ellingham could be your tutor. You might one day take over that position."

"That's certainly a generous offer, sir. I have to be honest and tell you that my real interest is my tour business. And I would miss my Beth."

That last sentence disturbed Al-Aziz, but didn't let it show. He had not counted on a Beth. He had other plans for Hank.

The next morning, accompanied by Ali and two of his personal guards, Al-Aziz took Hank out for a hunt. Their quarry was Barbary deer. He maintained a stock of the native species on his lands. All five set out on horseback. Hank's mount was now a chestnut. He assumed that the dappled gray was due for grooming and a well-deserved rest.

Hank and Ali left their sidearms in their quarters. What need would they have for them on a hunting expedition? They would both soon regret that decision.

"I will take you out in my Leyland Motor Car tomorrow. It is not at all suitable for hunting. Scares off the deer or anything else with an ear and sense of survival to it, including people." In a jovial mood he continued, "If you shoot straight, we will have venison for the main course at dinner tonight," Al-Aziz teased. They never got the chance.

They spotted the empty carriage, devoid of horses and with the dead bodies of the escorts alongside. Al-Aziz was the first to spur his horse at a gallop. The others quickly followed. Hank had a brief flashback but seriously doubted that ambushers lie in wait, hiding beneath the ground.

"This was all my fault. Allah, forgive me." Al-Aziz cried out. No one in the party understood the outburst. "My Jasmina has been taken. If any harm comes to her, I will personally cut off the balls of the perpetrators." There were signs everywhere of many horses. The trail ran west toward the Rif.

What the distraught father did not tell them was that he planned what would have appeared to be a chance encounter with his daughter in the presence of her chaperone. He had hoped to spark a romance. He did not think that an arranged marriage between Hank and Jasmina would appeal to the cowboy. It was not an American custom, at least as far as he knew.

"Ali, go now and track them. Take these two with you," he commanded, pointing to the other guards. "Mr. Miller and I will ride back and have General El Medhi assemble his cavalry. I will lead them myself."

"Sir, please, allow me a suggestion," Hank intervened. "It will take a hard ride to catch them murdering bandits before they can lose themselves in the mountains. Let me and Ali go after them. We'll have to run our horses into the ground. We can take your guards' horses as remounts. I once promised myself I would never run from a fight. I want to keep that promise in the here and now."

Although he implicitly trusted his own home guard, he knew Hank's reputation and saw the wisdom in his offer. Somewhere, though, in the back of his mind he also hoped that a rescue would be the spark to light the romance. He told his soldiers to get off their horses and give them to Hank and

Ali. They followed orders, one of them yielding his water sack and knife to Hank.

"Go with Allah." Nothing else need be said. The pair galloped to the west. Al-Aziz did the same to the east.

"I guess you saw the blood stains in the grass. The guards must have gotten a few of them before they died. I counted eleven men on horseback from their tracks," Hank called to Ali as they rode.

"Twelve," was all he said in response.

By the time they caught up to the kidnappers it was nightfall. They had spotted their campfires. Hank thought back to an earlier time when he had found the killers of his friend Charlie. Funny how the past catches up with you. You can't escape it, at least the parts you want to forget. He had once been wild with anger and rash in his actions. He was neither now.

Their Arabians were foaming at the mouth and would ride themselves to the death if they were pushed any further. They had abandoned their first mounts hours ago, just as they were about to collapse.

In a quiet voice Hank told Ali, "We had better leave the horses here. We'll tie them to that scrub tree over there. We can't push them any further, and we'll need them rested if we are to get out of this alive."

Ali led them up a ridge overlooking the encampment. The moon was almost full, giving them a good view of its layout. There were six small tents around a central campfire. They guessed that there would be no more than twelve or thirteen in the raiding party. The two of them kept their voices low. Sound carried out there into the valley below.

"These are arrogant or stupid men or both. Did they not think we would track them? Did they not think that their campfire was a beacon?" Ali questioned.

"Could be a trap."

"Of what kind? Would they want to be slaughtered by luring our whole army here?"

That did not make sense. They likely had seen an opportunity and taken it, figuring the well-dressed women, protected by guards, would be worth a hefty ransom. They probably had no idea who they had taken. Jasmina and her caretaker would be careful not to tell them. Better to lie. Identifying themselves might cost them their lives. The would-be kidnappers might fear the wrath of Al-Aziz and turn killers to leave no witness behind. Then, make a run for the mountains where they could disappear. No, that didn't add up either. Who in the Rif would not know they were on the property of the great Hasan Al-Aziz? None of this really made sense. They put aside speculation to focus on the task at hand. It would remain a mystery for over twenty years.

"That one there on the right," Ali pointed. "That must be the tent where they keep the little one. A man stands guard at its front."

They crept down the ridge the way they came and circled to the back of the tent where they believed Jasmina was held. Both paused to listen before Ali used his knife to slit the material. He held the flap open as Hank slipped in. He found the girl sleeping, curled on the ground. Hank crept to her and placed his hand over her mouth to prevent her from making noise. Jasmina instantly awoke, eyes wide with fear. She made a muffled sound. Hank had his back to the front of the tent and did not see the sentry enter, attracted by the noise and carrying his rifle at the ready. Hank turned in time to see a knife sticking out of the man's throat. The guard dropped the rifle and pitched forward, flopping to the ground. Blood was leaking out of the wound. It spurted on all of them as Ali retrieved his dagger.

Sensing her shock, Ali told Jasmina, "We must leave, *now*."

"No, I can't. Not without Rehana. She is in the next tent,"

Knowing that an argument would delay things and diminish their already slim chance of escape, he said, "All right. Hank take the little one to the horses. I will meet you there."

Hank took the girl by the hand and led her out the back of the tent into the darkness beyond. Ali followed but crept over to the back of the neighboring shelter. As he crawled he could see it was unguarded. Once again he used his knife to slit the canvas. Ali saw why no one stood guard. Rehana lay in a pool of blood, knife protruding from her abdomen and her traditional dress torn off at the waist. He slipped back out, quietly cursing the barbarians who could have done such a thing. Ali vowed revenge.

When he reached the horses, the other two were already there waiting. It was almost dawn. "Where is Rehana?" Jasmina asked.

"I'm sorry my little princess. She is gone." He turned to Hank and shook his head. No further questions should be asked now. Hank understood the meaning of the gesture. They mounted their still exhausted horses, Jasmina behind Hank, encircling his waist with her arms. They started off slowly to make as little noise as possible. Just then a shot rang out. They could hear shouts from the camp. They spurred their Arabians to a gallop.

Soon after, riders appeared from behind. They knew they had little chance of escape. Tired as they were, their horses could never outrun the cutthroats who chased them. Ali yelled, "I'll dismount. One of you take my horse. It will give you a better chance."

Hank and Jasmina together screamed, "No." They kept on riding. In moments they heard the crack of gunfire. Bullets began to hit the dirt around them. Then, they began to whiz by. They saw a hill up ahead with rocks on top that would provide at least some cover. They veered and headed for it. The horses struggled up the slope. Finally, they could go no further on horseback. Hank got off his mount and reached up to hoist Jasmina down by the waist. They removed their rifles from their scabbards and scrambled to the top. Bullets pinged off the rocky ground. Their pursuers were less than one hundred yards away.

By now the sun had risen well over the horizon. It gave them their sole advantage. It shone in the faces of the attackers, blinding them. They too had dismounted and were climbing the hill.

"Your father must be near by now," Hank said to Jasmina, as much to comfort her as to do the same for himself.

They were lying behind rocks. "I didn't expect to test your marksmanship in quite this way, Hank."

"Neither did I." Hank dearly wanted to put his hand in his left trouser pocket and squeeze that locket. He couldn't.

He needed them both to aim and shoot his rifle. His target came into sharp focus, like all the other men he had ever shot. For a second there was nothing else in the world apart from the man he was about to kill.

They fired and hit their intended victims, knocking them backward with the force of the impact. That stopped the advance, at least, for the moment. The pair kept up a steady stream of fire to keep the kidnappers pinned down. Their supply of ammunition was quickly running low. Hank had started with sixteen rounds and Ali ten. That was the number their rifles would carry. Neither had reloads. Nor did they have their sidearms. After all, who would use a Colt to hunt deer? And they faced another threat. Their attackers would eventually figure out a way around the hill to get behind them. They may have already.

To conserve what little ammunition they had left Hank and Ali paused in their shooting. Then, all three heard it, the sound of many pounding hooves. The outlaw band must have heard it too because they abandoned the attack and began to run down the hill. Hank and Ali hesitated at first, reluctant to shoot anyone in the back. Ali recalled what he had seen in Rehana's tent and was about to fire. So was Hank.

At that instant Al-Aziz and his general led a charge into the midst of the panicked kidnappers. They used their curved blades to chop the screaming men to pieces. There was no need for Hank or Ali to fire their weapons.

When it was over, they let the dead lie where they had fallen. They could not be true Muslims and did not deserve burial. Al-Aziz sent a few men back to retrieve the body of Rehana. They never told Jasmina what had happened. She never asked. But she never told *them* of the screams she heard coming from her beloved chaperone's tent.

That night they returned to the cheers of the local populace and the members of the staff who lined the road to the gates of the wall as well as the path to the palace itself. Hank and Ali were the first to pass through an honor guard that stood on both sides of that path. Al-Aziz for the first time in his adult life held back, riding alongside his daughter. Jasmina's mother rushed out to greet her, holding her in a fierce embrace after she dismounted. It was the first time they saw Jasmina cry. She had held it in until safely in her mother's arms.

The entire town of Zinat held a feast and gave thanks to Allah for saving Jasmina. The palace was lit up by torches ensconced, it seemed, everywhere outside. Tapers filled the chandeliers and the candelabras throughout the interior. Light gleamed from all the windows.

Hank and Ali were exhausted beyond words. They stood next to one another, gazing up at the stars from the side entrance that led to the dining room. It was the first time Ali had dined inside the palace. The one family member who did not thank him was Ahmed.

Al-Aziz came up from behind and clasped the pair on the back. "Thank you, gentleman. Words fail to express the depth of my gratitude. Hank, you have exceeded your own already prodigious reputation. A botanist, ha! That is no life for you. If you stay and marry my daughter, I shall make you rich beyond imagining."

Hank stiffened but did not respond. He had a feeling that Mr. Al-Aziz would get around to that sooner or later.

"Ali, you have proven yourself worthy. You shall succeed General El Mehdi when he retires. In the meantime I will send you off to the British for officer training." With that he retreated back to the dining room.

Hank was too tired to fully appreciate the implications of what his erstwhile father-in-law had said. Both he and Ali went off to sleep shortly thereafter. But not before they embraced. They had formed a lifelong bond that would transcend the distance between them. "Thank you Ali. Thank you for saving my life."

"No, the thanks is mine, my friend. Besides, how could I let a living legend not return to his sweetheart. Your Beth would never have forgiven me." They had shared the story of their lives earlier that night and knew one another better than they knew themselves.

The celebration lasted three days. Hank knew it was time to go.

Al-Aziz had a caravan assembled to escort him back to Tangier. It would be well guarded. Jasmina with her parents were there to see him off.

He was the first to speak. "Mr. Miller, Hank my friend, I could not save your soul. But I certainly can make your mortal life comfortable. May Allah in his infinite mercy protect you and bring you back to your Beth safe and sound." He handed him a small, nondescript chest and a separate key. It appeared to have been crafted from gold. "Guard this well. Do not under any circumstances open it until you are on board ship and alone in your cabin. I have arranged for staterooms on both of the ships you will take. You will find a crate inside the first. Do not let it out of your sight."

Jasmina with a tear rolling down her cheek merely said, "Thank you." Whatever else she meant to say stuck in her throat. Twenty-one years later she would take the opportunity to pay back the same men for having saved her life.

Hank said his farewell. "I'm obliged for your hospitality Mr. Al-Aziz. Thank you for having invited me here to your home. It is fit for a king, and a royal in heart you truly are. And thank you for the gift."

Al-Aziz was impressed with Hank's words. At least, he didn't always sound like a bumpkin someone set free from America's western frontier. In fact, he believed he finally understood his guest. Hank was a man eloquent in action, if not always in word.

Ali would accompany him to Tangier. He would arrange for his protection at the hotel and his safe passage to the White Star liner that awaited him at the dock. The first thing Hank did when he returned to Tangier was to send a cable to Beth, telling her he was safe and returning home. He knew her parents would forbid her to meet him in New York. But he hoped somehow, some way to see her and soon.

Neither man said much at their parting. There was no need. They assumed they would never again see one another. They clasped hands and remained that way for what seemed minutes. They owed each other their lives. What passed between them needed no words.

"May God protect you, General-to-be Ali. You have earned His affection."

"And may Allah watch over you, my friend."

Finally alone in his stateroom, Hank sat on the side of the bed and used the key to open the lock that guarded the

little chest. Inside he found gems, lots of gems. He took them
out one by one and placed them on the bed. There were five
diamonds, five rubies, five emeralds, five sapphires and five
of another jewel he could not identify: at first red, then,
aquamarine in color. The sunlight that streamed through the
porthole gleamed off them. They were dazzling in clarity.
And they all were large, very large. He would learn that five
of them were Alexandrite, the "emerald by day and ruby by
night," and the rarest, most astonishingly valuable of all.
Twenty-five gems, all in exquisitely cut in pentagonal shape.
Hank was dumbstruck. He glanced at the crate and wondered
what was inside. He did not yet know it was a vase of the
Ming dynasty, dating from the sixteenth century. Priceless, it
would one day stand as a mute sentry in the corner of the
entryway to his mansion on Nob Hill.

   Hank wrote a letter of thanks to his patron. He never received a reply. It was his courage that had earned him enormous wealth. It was by the grace of the Almighty that he survived yet another deadly encounter. But he had always
considered himself lucky. Now he thought he might be
blessed in a way other than luck. Not because he was worthy.
No, it was because he was given the means to protect others
worthy of protection. He had been given the responsibility
for protecting the lives of innocents. His failure to prevent
Charlie's and Jim's murders still weighed heavily. He, himself,
had killed in the past and now had again. Hank wanted no
more of killing. He would have to find a way to share his luck
other than through violence. Hank would eventually find that
way in a city devastated by nature's wrath, six thousand miles
and fifteen years away.

People always wondered where he and Beth had gotten the money to expand their business and build their home. No one outside the family ever found out.

Chapter 17:
Zinat, Morocco. July 28, 1912

(The Present)

The Attempt

As Hank spotted the palace at Zinat it brought back memories of a time twenty or so years ago when he had in fact accomplished a rescue. It had been a harrowing experience. It was one that had brought him unimaginable riches. It was also one that had brought with it an enduring friendship and a debt that had to be paid.

Soldiers on horseback rode out to meet their party. Their uniforms had changed. They no longer sported blue jackets atop the loose-fitting outfits of the past. And rather than greet them as an honor guard they simply surrounded them. This was not an auspicious start.

Hank leaned over in his saddle and whispered to his son David who rode beside him, "Not a right friendly reception."

Right on cue and without a word of greeting the leader began, "I am Yousef, commander of the Army of Pasha Ahmed Al-Aziz. You are to accompany me to the palace."

Hank decided it was best not to challenge the title of Pasha which did not apply. The Sultan of Morocco was the only one who could bestow the title, and he had not done so. Egomaniac that he was, Ahmed had appropriated it for himself.

And he thought to himself, "Well, where else would we be going, son?" Hank, always the diplomat, held his tongue. Well, almost always, when it suited his purposes. He was there to effect a rescue, not antagonize the leader of a group of over twenty heavily armed men.

They followed Commander Yousef through the massive gates that opened into the palace courtyard. The last time he had done so, it was to a raucous celebration. This time he hoped it wouldn't end in a silent wake. No throngs were there to cheer the men who had saved Jasmina, the youngest daughter of Hasan Al-Aziz. Tradesmen, servants, workers of all sorts went about their business, keeping their heads down. It was odd they didn't show any curiosity toward the new arrivals. Times sure had changed out here and not for the better.

The date palms still lined the path along the front of the palace, but no longer seemed a part of the pageantry that greeted visitors. They looked more like sentries armed with fronds.

The four of them got off their horses while the rest of the caravan waited for instruction. The two guides and mule riders remained mounted.

Yousef pointed to four of the servants, "Take care of the animals and men." It was an imperious command. Turning to Hank, "Which are the crates with the merchandise?"

"The first four mules." His reply was terse. Hank did not appear to like this man.

Figgins added, "Keep the crates with the ammunition boxes stored in a cool place."

"Remove your gun belts, gentleman. None but the royal guard may enter the palace armed. They will be returned to you when you depart." It was the last thing he said before motioning them to go ascend the stairs.

They did as instructed and mounted the steps to the palace doors. As had been done countless times before, the waiting servants opened them for the visitors.

As he entered Hank recalled the sense of wonder he had first experienced at the sight of the interior. He could not help marvel at the grand foyer, leading to the staircase that seemed to climb to the heavens.

"No boys, don't get yourselves too distracted by these surroundings. Keep in mind the mission." As part of the planning for that mission he had already sketched out the general layout in case they would have to make a hasty departure. They had all memorized it.

David and Ben could not help but stare at the wonder that stood before them. Before any of them could say anything else, a small man in red livery approached.

"I am Omar. I will escort you to the Pasha."

The four of them followed him into the reception room. After bowing to his master, he withdrew as discreetly as he had entered. Two guards closed the doors and stepped to either side of them.

As Hank scanned the chamber, he saw Ahmed sitting in a throne-like chair on a dais straight ahead. None of that had been there before. And all the chairs had been removed. Ali and Amina stood off to the side, silent and unmoving, father clutching his daughter.

"Ah, welcome Mr. Miller and your sons. Figgins, is it?" Ahmed did not stir from his seat. He did have a smile on his face, but it was not a welcoming one. It was more like that of a predator.

They fanned out in a line to face him. They hoped he was the quarry and not them. But at that point it was not at all clear who was the hunter and who the hunted.

"Let's get down to business, Ahmed," Hank began.

"Yes, let's." He started off in solicitous fashion, but abruptly changed to a strident voice. "First of all, you are to address me as Pasha Ahmed or Your Eminence. I am not some backwater potentate you Americans or Brits can scoff at. Do not look down your noses at me. When I am sultan," he paused there, realizing he had gone too far. His egomania posed a threat to the entire country. "My father had me instructed by the best British and French tutors he could buy. Mais oui? Commençons, mes amis."

"Well, Mr. Pasha Your Eminence, we here done brung what you wanted. Now it's your turn. Hand over them folks over there, and we'll be on our way." Hank had his hand in his left pocket gripping the ever-present locket. No need to tempt his luck. He nodded to Ali, making brief eye contact with him. Ali did not respond in kind. He stood there, tense, fear radiating from his eyes.

Clearly something was amiss. Couldn't their father see that? The twins were disturbed. Greatly so. But they didn't let it show or believed they didn't. They both thought back to that cryptic remark Hank had made about rehearsing his lines. Could that have anything to do with what he was saying now? Ben and David could not understand why their father had lapsed into a faux western drawl. What purpose could it serve? Why he would want to antagonize a man who held all their lives in his hands. Was he really trying to rile up this maniac? Really? The guards behind them had rifles slung on their shoulders and long curved blades in scabbards on their belts. Beyond that a whole army stood between them and Tangier. And Figgins had said nothing. What was going on?

Addressing Hank, Ahmed responded, "Ah you want to leave my humble palace so soon, do you? Does that also apply to your boys or Figgins?" He was clearly toying with them. "What is to stop me from taking that Maxim of yours and killing all of you? After all, it would come as no surprise that four foreigners would simply vanish in the Rif. We might even arrange for an elaborate ruse and send a demand for ransom to your wife, that is, after we killed you. Could we not, my old friend, *Hank*?"

As cool as a cucumber, Hank replied, "Well sir, who's to say we brung all the parts you need to assemble that gun. We could've left them behind in Tangier for your men to pick up once we arrived back in safety."

"An obvious bluff. You are no good at poker, Hank. Try your luck at a game you know how to play. This is not it."

Now it was Figgins' turn to speak up. "It is no bluff. That is exactly what we did."

That certainly gave Ahmad pause. However, he recovered quickly. "Let us say that you did leave a crucial part behind. Perhaps I should ask you politely where you hid it. Or perhaps I would ask you after I had the eyes plucked out of one of your sons." Lazily, he turned his gaze on the boys. "How would you like that, young gentlemen? Which one of you volunteers to be first?"

Ben and David stiffened, but said nothing. Some kind of game was being played here. But they didn't know what it was. Had their father, who had sworn to protect them, been so easily outwitted?

"I never told you what really happened to Jasmina, my beloved *sister*. I have no need to withhold that secret from dead men. Those raiders were meant for my father and you, *Hank*. I knew that he planned that outing of hers to be along the route he would take on the hunt. She knew, too. Dutiful daughter that she was. She would follow instructions and flutter those big brown eyes of hers. It was meant to appear as a chance encounter to start a romance with you, leading to marriage. He would have undoubtedly provided you with other irresistible enticements besides the body of my sister. You would have to convert first, of course, *infidel* that you are. You would have had to learn to speak English. Something you have yet to master. You still sound like a hayseed idiot. *You* would have become his favorite, not me. Those fools were supposed to kill you *and* my father. But they found *her* first and panicked. I promised them riches. I admit that I would have had them killed. You and my father took care of that at least. Thank you. Dead men tell no tales. And neither will any of you."

Hank looked startled at first. He never understood how anyone could not know they were on the lands of Hasan Al-Aziz when they kidnapped the girl. How could they not at least guess who she was? Finally, it all made sense.

Recovering, he asked, "And how do you plan to assemble the Maxim without Figgins?"

"Oh, he'll do it. Won't you Figgins? I've paid you enough, haven't I?"

"Yes, of course, Sir."

***

As if on cue a knock came to the doors. Ahmed nodded his approval for his guards to open it. Commander Yousef appeared, bearing the gun belts he had previously confiscated and a pack. "Your Eminence, I have brought their weapons as you instructed."

"What are you talking about?" Ahmed was visibly annoyed. "I gave no such order."

At that, the guards shut the doors.

"Yousef, take those guns out of here. *Now*. We will have a talk later."

Instead, he handed them to the four men. He also took out four djellabas from his pack. "Put these on. They will hide your weapons." The twins appeared as baffled as Ahmed.

"What do you think you are doing, Yousef?" Anger and panic seized him. "I will have your hands cut off and stuffed in your mouth for this. Guards, take those belts away."

Neither moved.

Hank smiled for the first time. "If you make another sound, Yousef here is going to slit your throat." Ahmed quieted as his commander approached with his jambiya in hand. His eyes were wide with fear and disbelief.

"Ali, Amina, come here," Hank instructed.

He turned to his twins, "I'm sorry boys. There's no time to explain. You had to look genuinely frightened. I didn't know if you were good actors. We couldn't take a chance. You had to show real fear. And we needed Ahmed to keep talking until Yousef arrived. We couldn't have him getting us killed until reinforcements got here."

Hank and Ali exchanged a brief embrace, patting each other on the back.

Ali placed a hand on his daughter's shoulder, "Everything is going to be ok now, my love."

Hank smiled reassuringly at the youngster, but quickly focused on the task at hand. This was no time for introductions or conversation. The group turned toward the door, led by Yousef, followed by Ahmed with Hank right behind, nudging him forward with the muzzle of the Colt hidden under his light overgarment. The boys, Figgins, and Ali with Amina were next in line. The two guards brought up the rear.

They had done well so far. Everything had gone according to plan. Now it was time to move. If their deception were uncovered, it would mean death to them all.

Once outside, Yousef shouted orders. "Have the Pasha's favorite mount brought immediately. Bring horses for these two," he called, pointing to the former door guards. "Pack supplies and the Pasha's tent. *Quickly. Move.*" Servants scrambled to obey.

Before they could depart, however, Omar the majordomo appeared at the palace doorway and rushed down the steps. "Your eminence, I apologize. I did not know you intended to travel."

Keeping a smile on his face was hard, but Hank managed it as he poked the gun into Ahmed's back. "Remember," he whispered, "Figgins is fluent in Arabic."

"It is nothing Omar. I have decided to go to my villa outside of Tangier. I have business there with these gentlemen. They want to purchase several of my Arabians. Ali and his runt are part of the bargain. They want them as servants. I have no need of those dogs any longer." And in a softer tone, "Have no worry, Omar. These men will accompany me, and I have Yousef and these two for protection. Who would dare to try to harm me?"

The staff were used to their ruler's whims, but this was unusual even for him. Hank kept the barrel pressed against him.

"Good thinking, Ahmed, very convincing," whispered Hank into his left ear. "Keep it up and we will all come out of this alive. Why we might even find you a part as the jester in *King Lear.*"

Ahmed had no idea what Hank was talking about, but he did comprehend that his life depended on keeping up the charade. It took a highly uncomfortable thirty minutes to reassemble the caravan. Record time it was. No one wanted to risk the wrath of the self-declared pasha.

They departed ever so slowly. It seemed the length of a long Texas summer day before they all passed through the gates of the compound. Hank rode closely behind Ahmed, his gun pointed at the small of his back. The rest followed.

A half hour later Ahmed turned to Hank, "I will have your head for this, you pig. How dare you do this to me."

"I have done nothing to you, little pasha, that you didn't rightly deserve. I kept my part of the bargain and left the Maxim behind. As for my head, I'd worry more about yours than mine. I swear by all that is holy that if any harm comes to my boys or the rest of this party, you will never make it back to your palace. I swear it." Hank cantered ahead, leaving Figgins to watch over their captive.

Ahmed remained silent after that.

The boys rode up to their father, flanking him. Ben was the first to register a protest. "Pops, I can't believe you did that to us. How could you?"

"Yeah Pops, you really couldn't trust us?" Ben added, righteously aggrieved.

"It wasn't either of you I couldn't trust. It was your acting skills. Remember that play of yours in the fifth grade, *A Christmas Carol?* You both forgot your lines. I couldn't take the chance you might forget again. Besides, I already told you. I had to make sure you looked genuinely frightened."

"We had no lines to forget this time, Pops," they said in unison.

"But I did. When we first encountered Raisuli on the way to Zinat I said we weren't going to surrender. But I said it in my best West Texan. I told you I was 'rehearsing.' I really was. I couldn't afford to forget *my* lines. This was no children's play I was practicing for. I had to make sure I could speak in that old way of mine when we confronted Ahmed. I needed to provoke him in order to keep him distracted long enough for Youssef to arrive."

"You sure did that," Ben replied.

"Well, that's the truth, ain't it?" Hank said no more and neither did the twins.

They made camp early that evening. The father and son duo that had been their guides rode ahead to alert the crew of *The Beth* to be ready for immediate departure. Hank and Figgins thought it best not to linger in Tangier. No, that would not be a good idea at all.

After the porters erected his tent, Figgins brought Ahmed inside and securely tied him to the middle post. One of the palace door guards went in to feed him later. They had made good time traveling. All in all, it had been a good day.

Before settling down by the cooking fire, the boys took their father aside. David was the one to speak. "Pops, this may not be the best time to ask. Or maybe it is. But both of us have been wondering. What was it about mom that attracted you in the first place? Apart from the obvious that she was beautiful."

Little did they know that six thousand miles away their sister had asked the very same question of their mother.

Hank was caught off guard. He had many times praised their mother to their children, but had never discussed what he considered private matters. And this was a private matter. Nevertheless, he realized he might never again have the opportunity to tell the twins an important part of his history. Their collective history.

He was pensive for a moment and then a wide grin spread across his face as he recalled their first encounter.

"When your mother stepped out of her train car, she looked regal. I think that's the right word. Her bearing was nothing short of aristocratic. At the time I would have said that she cut a fine figure of a woman." Hank stopped there momentarily.

He had a look of wonder on his face. "But it was her eyes. Blue. Radiant blue. That's what I saw first. I couldn't help but stare. Something passed between us. I can't describe it. It lasted a second or two. I didn't understand it then, and still don't quite now.

"It was three days later that I learned that my Beth, Miss Elizabeth at the time, had grit. Real grit. She was much more than a spoiled, pretty girl from back East. You already know that. It took a life-or-death encounter for me to realize it. I admit, I can be mighty slow at times.

"Watching her walk up the steps to the train, ready to depart, I didn't think I'd ever see her again. She told me she hoped to see me in the future. I thought that was her being polite. But when my Beth turned back to wave before she got on board, I got that same feeling as when I first locked eyes with her. As I said before, I didn't know what it might mean at the time." He paused. "Or if it meant anything at all.

"If your mother hadn't started writing me those letters, you boys wouldn't be here today."

Yousef joined the four companions for dinner that night. At Hank's urging he disclosed his part in the deception. He was second cousin to Jasmina. They had spent their childhood and adolescence together. Jasmina and Yousef remained friends and shared a secret ever since that time together. They both detested Ahmed. She had sent a letter to Yousef in June, requesting that he come to Tangier to discuss a matter of great importance. He made some excuse and went.

It was at Jasmina's house that she made the offer: a position in her husband's household and a substantial pay raise, a really substantial one, for playing the part of loyal retainer. He readily agreed. It wasn't just the money or the deep dislike of Ahmed that motivated him. Yousef wanted to save Ali and Amina. The general had always been kind to him as a child whenever assigned to safeguard his welfare. He could barely hide his feelings thinking about the treatment meted out to his former guardian. It was deplorable. And it could happen to him one day.

For Youssef it was an easy task to find two guards willing to take bribes and to have them assigned guard duty at the doors to the reception room for the week of Hank's anticipated arrival. He had sent his wife and two daughters to Jasmina a month ago for a summer vacation. Nothing out of the ordinary. And Jasmina had sent a letter by special courier to Figgins, outlining the arrangement.

Hank and Ali sat next to one another during the meal. Ali thanked them all as did Amina. They spent their time together catching up and allowing Amina to chatter away. Ali beamed at the rapid recovery of the youthful exuberance she had lost during their captivity. In fact, her excited telling of it amused them all. But they weren't aboard ship yet, and clear sailing wasn't to be.

***

In Zinat, Alia had been combing the palace in search of her son. She finally summoned Omar and demanded to know where he was.

She grew increasingly agitated as the majordomo explained what had transpired. "He would never have left so suddenly and without telling me. And you say that Yousef took a mere two guards. What nonsense is that! Call that second-in-command whatever his name is. Have him assemble a suitable escort and go after them. Something is wrong. *Go.*"

***

The next day they spotted a few riders on the ridges above them. This time the horsemen waved in recognition to the party below. Raisuli was true to his word and apparently had sent an escort to see them safely back to Tangier.

The rest of the time the band of refugees from Zinat rode along in the comfortable silence of trusted comrades-in-arms. Beth was never far from Hank's thoughts. He just never spoke about them. Some things he kept private, even from his children. "I miss that gal something fierce," he thought. "Fierce enough to stay alive to have her in my arms again. Now that's a pleasant thought. Haven't had too many of those lately. And I do miss that little Rachael. Well, not so little anymore. She grew fast as a speeding locomotive. I think she must have skipped a few years, like she did in school. Went directly from nine to seventeen, she did."

Figgins intruded into Hank's reverie. "They're following us. Look behind you."

And there it was, an ominous cloud of dust. It was approaching too fast for a caravan. Had to be riders. Almost, almost, they had gotten away scot-free.

The five of them formed a circle with their horses. "The way I see it, we have two choices, fight or try to bluff our way out of it," said Figgins, drawing on his military experience. "There's no cover, unless we try for the top of that hill. No doubt they would eventually flank us. Who knows how many there are. Or how many would eventually reinforce them. No, our best option is to trot out that despicable Ahmed and pray he hasn't grown a spine. Our survival depends on his cowardice. No doubt Yousef will play his role well. All we can do is hope that will be enough."

There was no objection. They would continue on in an unhurried pace to avoid arousing suspicion. There was no way they could outrun the soldiers on horseback anyway.

Hank sidled up to Ahmed. "Looks like your cavalry is coming. But make no mistake. They will not rescue you. You will be the first to die if you do not continue to play along. But I pledge to you as a father that we will let you go, when we leave Tangier. Try to signal to your soldiers and you will be the first to die. I guarantee it."

Each of the men undid the flap covering their guns in their holsters but made no other threatening moves.

Yousef was the first to turn his horse to greet the soldiers. His second-in-command saluted, awaiting orders. "What is this Elhabib? Who authorized this?"

"Commander, mother of the Esteemed One ordered us to catch up with you. She sensed something was amiss."

"Does anything look amiss, Elhabib?"

"No sir. It does not."

At the most inconvenient of times, Ahmed grew that spine of his. Or maybe it was panic that motivated him. They never knew.

"You idiots. Can't you see they are kidnapping me?"

Time stood still. The two groups of riders stared at one another, until Elhabib went for his holstered Mauser. A shot echoed from the distance as he was thrown from the saddle, a bullet hole in his chest. Both groups looked to the source of the sound. It was the ridge to the north. There sat a bearded figure on a majestic black Arabian stallion holding President Roosevelt's Winchester aloft. With him were a large contingent of riders lined up all along the ridge. Had they first looked to the south, they would have seen a similar number on the opposite crest.

It was Yousef who spoke first. "Sergeant, take your men back to Zinat. No more killing need be done today. No harm will come to the Pasha. I promise."

Eyeing the forces arrayed against them, the sergeant decided that discretion was the better part of valor. "Yes, sir." He then told his men, "Put away your rifles. Gather up Elhabib. We return to Zinat." He turned his horse and led his force away.

Hank took his hand out of his left pocket where he had kept it during the entire encounter. He removed his Stetson and lifted it in the air in salute to the man on the hill who had saved their lives. Raisuli returned the gesture, rearing his horse on its hind legs.

"I've always been lucky," Hank said aloud to no one in particular.

The remainder of the trip was uneventful. They reached Tangier on July Fourth. It was fitting, for they had freed innocents from captivity. The four of them quickly boarded *The Beth*. Hank and Figgins immediately sent a brief coded message to their respective families, "Lucky." It would be greeted with immense joy and flowing tears.

Yousef and his two soldiers had already departed for Jasmina's estate. They would be safe there. No one, not even Ahmed, would dare attack anyone under the protection of her husband, cousin to Sultan Abd al-Hafid ben Hassan.

They boarded quickly, leaving the horses and pack mules behind. The guides and workers under their employ appreciated the gift.

Ahmed, however, seemed unable to appreciate the gift that Hank had bestowed upon him ... his life. Ali was sorely tempted to slip a knife between that man's ribs but knew that his friend had made a pledge. They had made it back safe and sound. Ahmed would be released as promised.

As he stood there on the quay, the erstwhile pasha shouted to the departing steamship. Shaking his fist in the air, he yelled "I will never forget what you have done to me."

Now Hank had the last word, "I expect you won't." He turned away.

That night they gathered at the Captain's Table for dinner, minus the captain, of course. They had secrets to keep.

David put down his soup spoon. "You sure gave us a scare Figgins when that overblown rooster said you would put the Maxim together for him. And when you answered, 'Yes, of course, sir,' we were in shock. We thought you really had betrayed us."

Figgins responded, "That was the point, wasn't it? To scare the two of you. Had to be realistic. We were playing to an audience of one. And speaking of betrayal, I have a confession to make."

They all halted their eating, fearful of what would come next.

"I couldn't be loyal to you, Hank, and a traitor to my country. I couldn't offer up a weapon of incredible destructive power to a brigand with aspirations of grandeur. Delusions really. But no matter. My acquaintances in the army, although willing to take a bribe, couldn't either. So we rigged the cooling system to malfunction. The gun will overheat and jamb without it properly working. They timed how long it would take. One minute and twenty seconds of fire did it every time. Nonetheless, I had to be absolutely certain that the Maxim would fail. I had them take one other precaution.

"Remember that it fires 600 rounds a minute. That would be 800 in one minute twenty seconds, would it not?" He again paused theatrically and continued when the rest of the party nodded their assent. "I had them spike the ammunition with phosphorus, starting at shell number 750 and continuing to 900. A jolly job of it they did." He then halted his explanation, waiting for the implications to sink in.

"Don't stop there, Figgins. Go on man." This time it was Ben who had not yet figured it out. The rest had and smiled.

"The heat will cause the rounds with the phosphorus to explode, destroying the gun and likely killing or at least seriously wounding those manning it. It would overheat at one minute and twenty seconds at the 800th round. As I said, to be safe, we spiked the shells, starting at number 750 and continued through 900. It gave us a margin of safety. Couldn't have a madman acquire a taste for machine guns, now could we?"

They all looked at him in amazement. How could one man be so clever?

Instructing the captain of *The Beth* to store those "tomatoes" in a cool area and the near command at Zinat to do the same, the extra insulation, that odd umbrella-like contraption to shield the ammunition crates all finally made sense. Figgins might have any number of idiosyncrasies, but making sure what amounted to a heat sensitive bomb being safely stored was not one of them.

***

Two months later two mercenaries arrived in Zinat. They reassembled the Maxim but as expected failed to notice the alterations Figgins and his conspirators had made. Ahmed insisted on being the first to try it. He was buried the next day. Few mourned his passing.

Epilogue

Jasmina beamed when she received word of the successful rescue. She had relieved her debt and played her part in saving the lives of two worthy people. And she smiled with satisfaction at the demise of her half-brother. He deserved no better. She wistfully mused about what a life with Hank Miller might have been like. But Jasmina was content with hers. Oh, and by the way the two guards Yousef bribed to betray Ahmed … She had them killed. How could you ever trust such scum?

Ali would be safely settled in the New York office, working as a travel agent. There he would meet Miriam Gold, a refugee like himself who worked as a janitor at the agency. Her husband had died several years before, leaving her with three children to raise on her own. They married and had two more. He would retire at age seventy-six with twelve grandchildren, half practicing one faith and half another.

Julia would live to be one hundred and one years old. She would live to give innumerable hugs and kisses to her four children, twelve grandchildren, thirty-two great grandchildren, and ninety-three great, great grandchildren. She never remarried.

By the time she retired, Julia had taught more than one thousand students. For her one hundredth birthday many of them returned to San Antonio, gathering with family and friends to celebrate. Hank, fifteen years her junior, and Beth, joined them in the festivities.

Colonel Figgins would remain manager of the London office for two additional years. He took the job as president of the London Stock Exchange, a venerable financial institution of over one hundred ten years when he assumed command. He and his family prospered. Beth and Hank would visit on their annual pilgrimage to Great Britain and the continent. Those visits became fewer and fewer as they aged. The Colonel and Hank would regularly correspond for the rest of their lives.

Ben, David and Rachael had often discussed one day opening their own law firm together in San Francisco. It would have to wait as the choices they made and international events overtook their ambitions.

After graduating from college, **David** chose to join the U.S. Marshall's Service. As luck would have it, he was assigned to the Southwest Border Region and landed in the San Antonio office. His legal career would have to wait. He met a fine young woman, Rebecca Kaiser, and had two lovely girls. When World War I came knocking on America's door he was twenty-four. He joined the marines as a first lieutenant.

Ben opted for a different route. He enlisted in the army right out of college and was immediately chosen for Officer's Training School. His Harvard education, though, would be a hindrance to further advancement; he had not attended West Point. Ben, too, would be called to war. He and his young bride would spend only a week together before he shipped off.

Rachael would go on to attend law school. She married late for the era she grew up in. She was twenty-five. Rachael never anticipated her own role in the momentous and tragic events of the early twentieth century that would place her own family in enormous peril. Her life would take many turns, some through unexpected danger and others through unanticipated love.

Elizabeth was thrilled when three paintings by Matisse arrived in the fall of 1912. Years later, she would be the one to carry out the negotiations for the merger of two huge conglomerates: their own *The American West Touring Company* and *International Express Tours*. It came within a hair of running afoul of the Sherman Antitrust Act but made it through intact. She would be the first female CEO of an enterprise of that scale.

Beth formed a book club of two. She and Hank would enjoy discussing their readings for the rest of their lives. She never stopped correcting her husband's grammar.

Returning from Morocco for a second time, **Hank** found the transition back to civilian life, so to speak, a difficult one. His appetite for adventure had been rekindled. As a diversion he took up running marathons, having read of the exploits of the great Jim Thorpe in the Swedish Olympics of 1912. His physique was not ideal for running. He had become slightly bow legged from all those years atop horses. And he was a bit muscular to be a fast distance runner. Nevertheless he persevered as he did with everything else in his life, achieving a personal best of a few minutes under four hours for the

24.2-mile course. After the Great Earthquake of 1906, he and Beth poured much of their fortune into rebuilding the city. As with virtually everything else they did, their good works turned into a real estate empire. Strange how things work out. Already immensely wealthy, helping others had made them among the richest families in America. The original source of that wealth would forever remain a closely held family secret.

Every now and then, Hank purposely lapsed in his grammar, allowing his wife the pleasure of dutifully correcting him. He kept up his writing. It would one day be published as a popular memoir, augmented by Beth's recollections. Few who read it, however, really believed that one man could have done so much in a single lifetime. They read it as entertaining fiction. There were a number of people around the world, however, who knew better ... as did their children and children's children. Despite his vow to never to leave his family again, fate had other things in store for Hank. Duty would call one more time.

The People

Hank Samuel Miller "Hank" – Main character

Elizabeth Louise Astor Miller "Beth" – Hank's wife

David Solomon Miller – Elder twin son

Benjamin William Miller – Younger twin son

Rachael Anne Miller – Daughter

Anna Miriam Müeller – Hank's mother

Karl Müeller – Hank's father

Elizabeth Agnes Astor Franklin – Beth's mother

Joseph Benjamin Franklin – Beth's father

Edgar James – Headmaster of Hank's boarding school

Emmanuel Clement – Leader of band of cattle thieves

Jeff Ake – Gunslinger and Hank's early advisor near El Paso

Charlie Breen – Hank's friend and mentor in Laredo

Zebulon Pickett – Ranch owner outside of Laredo

Mr. Hatigrove – Drygoods store owner in Laredo

Mayor Root – Mayor of Laredo

Mr. Gregg – Businessman in Laredo

Hattie MacDonald – Hank's girlfriend in Laredo

James Handy "Jim" – Blacksmith; Hank's friend and partner in San Antonio

Julia Handy – Jim's wife and school teacher

Mrs. Jane Dundee – Friend of Hank's mother near Castle Hills

Edgy Lamont – Cook for Hank's tour company in San Antonio

Martha Albright – Hank's secretary in San Antonio

Cole the Younger Younger – Outlaw leader near El Paso

Joe Bass – Part of the Younger Younger gang

Sam Bass – Gunslinger and brother of Joe

Arizona Bass – Outlaw cousin of Joe and Sam

Robert T. Coleman – Outlaw and partner of Arizona Bass

Colonel Archibald Figgins – Former officer of the British army

The Honorable Abdul Al-Aziz – Scion of the Al-Aziz Clan of Zinat, Morocco

Ahmed Al-Aziz – Son of Mr. Al-Aziz

Jasmina Al-Aziz – Daughter of Mr. Al-Aziz

Ali El Hassan – Former commander of Mr. Al-Aziz's legion and Hank's friend

Yousef El Alaoui – Cousin of Jasmina and Ali's successor

Timelines

The Past

1860? Birth of Heinrich Samuel Müeller

June 19, 1866: Battle of Castle Hills

Fall, 1875: Heinrich Müeller is reborn as Hank Miller

1875–1877: Hank Runs with the Clement Gang

1877–1879: Hank Meets Charlie and Works for Wells Fargo

May 3, 1878: Charlie Is Killed and Hank Metes Out Justice

1879–1882: Hank Works for Mr. Pickett

Summer, 1882: Hank Becomes Sheriff of Laredo

June 5, 1883: Hank Shoots Sam Bass

Fall, 1887: Hank Founds *The American West Tour Company*

September 2, 1888: Hank Finds Jane

April 10, 1890: Elizabeth Arrives

April 13, 1890: Jim and Tom Murdered; Hank and Elizabeth Deliver Justice

Fall, 1891: Hank Rescues Jasmina in Morocco and Acquires Riches

February 5, 1892: Elizabeth Louise Astor Franklin and Hank Samual Miller Wed

1893: Hank and Beth Move to San Francisco; Twins, David and Ben Arrive

1895: Rachael Joins the Family

April 18, 1906: Great San Francisco Earthquake

The Present

May 7, 1912: Ali's Letter Arrives

June 29, 1912: Hank and the Boys Depart San Francisco by Train

July 2, 1912: The Three Arrive New York City

July 4, 1912: Father and Sons Depart NYC for Liverpool via *The Beth*

July 10, 1912: They Arrive in Great Britain

July 12, 1912: The Trio departs for Morocco via *The Beth*

July 18,1912: Figgins Meets Them in Tangier

July 22, 1912: The Expedition Sets Off for Zinat

July 23, 1912: First Encounter with Raisuli

July 28,1912: They Arrive in Zinat and Depart with Ali, Amina and Ahmed

July 29, 1912: Raisuli Saves Them

August 2, 1912: They Reach Tangier and Steam Home

Author's Note

This is a work of historical fiction. The story had been rattling around my brain for a dozen years. What prompted me to finally put pen to paper, I cannot say. Perhaps it was my failure as a cub reporter, an attempt at a second career after retiring as a physician. I liked writing and now had an impetus to continue, just in a different format. I had become attached to the characters living upstairs in my brain for so long. As you might have guessed Hank was and is a particular favorite of mine. In a way he became part of my family. I had told his yarns to many hiking partners over the years. I did so in a facsimile of the accent and wording I imagined an early version of Hank would have used. Perhaps that is why some of them chose not to accompany me again on one of those long treks.

I did my best to portray the spirit of the times and places in which I placed my friends. I aimed for accuracy in describing the actual physical appearance of the environs of their times: cities, towns, and landscapes as they were. Old photos were invaluable. I hope I captured their spirit reasonably well. At no time did I mean to disparage the idiom Texans might have used a century or so ago. I did live there for three years, although more than enough time had passed for that idiom to have shifted. I reckon I drew from the Westerns: movies and television shows I had watched as a kid and rewatched many times as an older adult with too much time on his hands. Zane Grey, Louis L'Amour, Larry McMurtry and Matt Dillon (the Marshal of Dodge City, not the actor) proved invaluable sources of inspiration.

I did my best to portray Tangier and the Rif with some reasonable accuracy. All I can say about that is that I did my research and blended in a fantasy of my own imagination.

Dear reader (as an author of a century and a half ago might have said), I hope you don't judge my literary references as mere affectation or my commentary as too superficial. I peppered the pages with those allusions and interludes to spice up the narrative and to demonstrate Hank's evolution as a writer. I readily admit that it has been many years since I had actually read the majority of the books and poetry I cited. I also hope my mention of those masterpieces kindle an interest in them. They describe the human condition in a provocative and insightful manner. Who knows, they might inspire the next great American novelist or help a doctor better understand human nature.

I will say that most of the real people who populate these pages were actually in the places at the times that Hank found himself passing through. Outlaws were an exception. I have no idea where they really were or what they were doing when Hank roamed the West. I merely borrowed their names.

Caruso, though, really was staying at the Plaza in San Francisco at the time the earthquake struck in 1906 and did perform at the Mission Opera House the night before. He escaped the destruction of the hotel unharmed. Matisse really was in Tangier in the spring of 1912. Raisuli was an outsized figure in his time with a well-earned, truly fierce reputation. Whether he was in the Rif in 1912, I confess, I don't know. Sean Connery portrayed him in a wonderful movie, *The Wind and the Lion*, also starring Candice Bergen. You should watch it.

Now that Hank and Beth and all the others are finally on paper, I can finally rest easy. My own burden of memory has been passed along to you.

About the Author

Jan is a retired physician living with his wife, a practicing pediatrician in Southern California. Their children have all flown the coop.